I0652143

Tribute To A Woman

Sentiments Of A Man

Tribute To A Woman

Sentiments Of A Man

Poetry by:

COREY LEIGH

Bren-Rose Publishing

New York, NY

Copyright © 2022 by Corey Leigh

All rights reserved. No part of this publication may be reproduced, distributed, or transmitted in any form by any means, including photocopying, recording, or other electronic methods without the prior written permission of the author, except in the case of brief quotations embodied in reviews and certain other noncommercial uses permitted by copyright law. To request permissions, contact the author at: sircoreyleigh@gmail.com

License Notes:

This eBook is licensed for your personal enjoyment. This eBook may not be re-sold or given away. No part of this publication may be reproduced, distributed, or transmitted in any form or by any means, including photocopying, recording, or other electronic or mechanical methods, without the prior written permission of the publisher, except in the case of brief quotations embodied in critical reviews and certain other noncommercial uses permitted by copyright law.

Paperback: ISBN 979-8-9853638-1-4
eBook: ISBN 979-8-9853638-4-5

Library of Congress Control Number: 2022900030

Printed and bound in the United States of America
First paperback edition: March 2022

Editor: Corey Leigh
Assoc. Editors: Melissa Cheng, Meesha Howard
Cover Art: Ana Marinovic
Book Layout: Word-2-Kindle
Photography: Vlad Satori

Bren-Rose Publishing
New York, NY

Dedication

To my late Mother, the incomparably incomparable, unequivocal queen of my heart, Ms. Brenda Love! As Langston Hughes famously penned, life for you was no crystal stair, yet, you always found the strength, exhibited the will, and exercised faith to continuously climb.

Lord knows, your example and countless sacrifices paved the way. I wouldn't be the man I am, less you the incredible woman you were.

Sadness envelopes me, and tears swell writing this, knowing you are no longer present, physically, to share in the monumental occasion of this accomplishment.

Simultaneously, a sense of gladness comforts my somber mood, remembering, you foresaw this very moment long before it ever came to be.

Eyes dry reassuringly, knowing you are beyond proud and celebrating in spirit, as this dream of mine, which you alone avidly encouraged, even when I doubted and lost faith, is now finally a reality.

You always told me, "Son, don't sit on your gift!" With that in mind, and on shoulders of all your love and support, I stand triumphant in its use.

Ceremoniously, with all the reverence I possess inside, I am honored to exclaim; my lifelong dream, this long-awaited, highly anticipated, first book of mine, in loving memory, is deservedly dedicated unto you.

May your spirit live forever! I love you Momma, always . . .

Definitions

trib·ute \ˈtri—(ˌ)byüt, —byət\

1

a: something given or contributed voluntarily as due or deserved; *especially*: a gift or service showing respect, gratitude, or affection

b: something (as material evidence or a formal attestation) that indicates the worth, virtue, or effectiveness of the one in question

sen·ti·ment \ˈsen—tə—mənt\

1

a: an attitude, thought, or judgment prompted by feeling

2

a: emotion

b: refined feeling: delicate sensibility especially as expressed in a work of art

c: emotional idealism

d: a romantic or nostalgic feeling verging on sentimentality

3

a: an idea colored by emotion

b: the emotional significance of a passage or expression as distinguished from its verbal context

Contents

Introduction: My First Poem(s)

I wrote my first poem in fifth grade when I was 10 years old. By first, I most certainly mean, my first poem that was actually any good! A lover of language arts and literature, as a child I wrote exceptionally well, including short stories, reports, essays, etc., but for some reason, poetry was difficult for me. I struggled with rhyme schemes, meter, and imagery, as well as the conciseness differentiating poetry from prose. Consequently, I stubbornly shunned all poetry writing assignments.

Without warning, one day, everything changed. In the weeks leading up to Black History Month that year, my teacher at the time, the brilliant and beautiful Ms. Karen Jones, decided to show our class the critically acclaimed miniseries, *Roots*. Once completed, our assignment was to write about what we saw, specifically, how it affected us.

Watching over the course of roughly two weeks, I contemplated drafting an introspective essay, one which would garner me an A grade. To aid in this, I took a mental note of various scenes I found emotionally riveting, startling, and to a larger degree, frightening.

The Friday afternoon we finished the series, we were given time to start the assignment in class, ahead of the weekend. Of both my seat and my emotions, I was on edge. Prior to that, I, like many of my classmates, had only heard stories about the horrors of slavery. None of us had seen such visual imagery, painfully depicting the plight, hardships, and dehumanization of our ancestors.

TRIBUTE TO A WOMAN

Officially allowed to begin, seemingly unable to control my pen, I scribbled wildly on the wide pages of my spiral notebook. I squeezed my erasable pen firmly, forcing its black ink between those white lines, intensely, against its will. My hand cramped achingly. I felt feverish, transferring ideas from the forefront of my mind to the blank page before me, as fast, and as accurately as possible.

So many emotions were bottled-up. On the verge of bursting, I attempted to write my pre-planned essay. However, I was amazed to discover in that moment, my sentiments had a mind of their own.

Once finished, I slammed my pen atop my desk. Slouching back in my chair, I exhaled audibly. It felt as if I held my breath that entire time. Gathering myself, I snatched up my notebook to read what I had written. To my complete surprise, a poem lay before me. A very descriptive, thoughtful, and perceptive piece of poetry.

Twice more, I reread it, searching for confirmation those words were actually mine. Admittedly impressed, a sense of pride enveloped me. Not only had I poetically articulated my thoughts and feelings, but I expressively captured the horror of historical events, witnessed during our 12-hour film session.

The following Monday, class resumed, and we read aloud our submissions. Regarded as class best, my poem would represent the fifth grade in performance at our annual Black History assembly. It was an absolute honor.

Ms. Jones had a brilliant idea to have a classmate, Latreace Lockhart, accompany me during recitation. Her oratory eloquence, plus mine, was a perfect pairing. Exchanging lines of each stanza, our back-and-forth added an even greater element to the piece.

COREY LEIGH

On the eve of the big day, Ms. Jones had laminated and gifted me a keepsake copy of my poem. An incredible gesture, I intended to remain in possession of it forever. Sadly, I have no idea what became of her gift. Eternally lost to me, I would give most anything to recover such a monumental, early work of mine. Year after year, I tried hard to recall each line from memory, regrettably, only ever able to retain the first few. They read:

> *We all remember black heroes*
> *Like Martin Luther King,*
> *And something they said*
> *Like, let freedom ring*
> *But in Africa,*
> *On a very special day*
> *A man-child was born,*
> *His name was Kunta Kinte*
> *Yes, Kunta Kinte was his name and,*
> *A Mandinka warrior he became . . .*

From there, I expressed how much Kunta meant to his family and his tribe, voicing their expectations of him to ascend as a leader, a warrior, and as a man of honor amongst his people. However, such dreams and aspirations went tragically unfulfilled. Eventually, he was kidnapped, stolen from his land and his loved ones, forever separated from each.

Addressing the dehumanizing nature of it all, I then touched on how slavery deprived him of his identity, heritage, cultural customs, and his dignity.

I concluded with how his impassioned spirit led him to attempt escape on several occasions, yet, hunted like an animal, in each instance he was recaptured, brutally beaten, and ultimately maimed in punitive fashion, to deter others from attempting the same. Ultimately, he resigned to endure the darkness of his bondage, hoping that brighter days of freedom would someday be afforded his daughter, and all descendants thereafter.

That was my first encounter harnessing such raw emotion, utilizing pure expression to produce a creative, specifically poetic, work of art. Like a drug, from that moment forth, I was fully addicted. Poetry immediately became my favorite form of self-expression.

Soon thereafter, Ms. Jones introduced me to the writings of American legend, Langston Hughes. *Dreams,* was the first of his I read, connecting to its message immediately. (Coincidentally, I recited it at an awards ceremony later that same year.) Langston became the catalyst for my subsequent desire to more maturely hone my skills, hoping to someday produce work capable of inspiring others, a wide-eyed child perhaps, much like myself, whose dreams of escaping the inner-city while using their own gifts to the best of their abilities, would someday become reality.

Fast forward two years, and I'm still a star pupil in the classroom, only this time, in a whole new atmosphere, at a whole new school, which in many ways, felt like a whole new world. Thanks to the persistent insistence of my mother, who always knew quality education would serve as an escape from our contentious urban environment, as well as a pristine record of continuous, high academic achievement, I gained acceptance and was enrolled into an affluent school district on Chicago's Northside. (A far cry from the grossly underfunded neighborhood schools, which unfavorable policy previously forced me to attend, my Westside residency a determining factor. A long-time Chicago practice I'll save my feelings toward for another day.)

In many ways, this was my first real look at the divide between the haves and have-nots, as well as an introduction to diversity, as both the students and staff there were of all ethnicities, cultures, and backgrounds. This exposure was one of the greatest occurrences of my life. It prepared and propelled me in so many ways, I could write a separate book on the value of that experience alone, but I digress.

Now, there I was in junior high, an extremely girl-crazy, sports obsessed, hip-hop influenced, somewhat self-conscious, and did I mention, extremely girl-crazy, know-it-all teen. Yet, in the midst of all things teenaged, I never stopped writing, particularly, my poetry.

More specifically, with all the girls I was then crushing on, I became solely focused on writing "love poems." I spent all available free time doing so, making it a point to finish in-class assignments and exams as early as possible, devoting the extra time to my poetry.

At that point, no one knew what I was up to. Occasionally, a classmate would ask what I was scribbling in my notebooks. Without hesitation I would openly lie and say I was writing rap lyrics. I was scared to death if my male classmates found out, despite being popular, I'd never live down their ridicule. Truthfully, I was even more afraid if any female counterparts discovered my secret, they'd laugh me to tears, which at that time, would've been the emotional equivalent of killing me.

As that year passed, I finally got the nerve to share my writing with a young lady I was especially interested in. She and I had recently

TRIBUTE TO A WOMAN

shared our first kiss, which by my logic meant, if she liked me enough to do so, she'd probably not make fun of my "lovey-dovey" poetry. Worth a shot, right?

Second-guessing, attempting to talk myself out of it, I found the fortitude and exercised resolve, refusing to chicken out. I recall sitting nervously at my desk that day, palms sweating, heart racing, waiting for the most opportune time to pass along a singular, handwritten, tri-folded page, otherwise known as a love note.

After what seemed like forever, our teacher, one of the most influential people ever in my life, the incredibly remarkable, Golden Apple award-winning, Mrs. Griselle Gemmati, had finally risen from her desk, which naturally overlooked the entire class.

She turned her back just long enough for me to rush out of my seat, and make my way two rows over to the desk of my fair lady, whose name I'll not reveal. Although, she wouldn't mind if I did, as we've discussed this occurrence fairly recently in fact, but something about it remaining our little secret after all these years, feels more appropriate.

All I know is, I exhibited poise under pressure. Mrs. Gemmati doesn't play, at all! Please believe, she'd have most certainly had my head on a decorative silver platter if she knew what I was up to. Sneaking behind her back was a huge no-no. If discovered, most assuredly, she'd have delighted in reading my letter aloud, for all the class, scratch that, all the school to hear! Afterwards, she'd have promptly phoned my mother and read it to her personally, furthering the swell of my embarrassment, while candidly explaining why my head now belonged to her.

Looking back, neither UPS nor USPS carriers could have made a quicker, stealthier, timelier delivery. In a flash, I was back in my seat sporting the calmest, "no-I-did-not-just-get-up-and-pass-a-note-behind-your-back," face of all time. Mission accomplished, sort of.

By then, the waiting game ensued. It was very much near the end of the school day, and I was hoping to have garnered a reaction before we departed, something to let me know how my words were perceived. The last thing I wanted was an hour-long bus ride, coupled with an entire evening at home in suspense, unsure of how she felt, clueless to what she thought.

Once again, I'm nervously at my desk, palms sweating and heart racing, watching the nearest wall clock. Class let out each day at exactly 3:15 PM. Five minutes prior, we were allowed to start packing up. Preparing to leave was always the most frenzied, chaotic time of the day. Including myself, many students were from various neighborhoods throughout the city. The last thing anyone wanted to be was the reason for a delayed departure. A school bus filled with kids, each overly eager to return home, was unforgiving to anyone who disrupted travel times.

As the clock reached ten-after, I told myself, it wasn't going to happen, I'd simply have to wait at least a day for her reaction. Soon thereafter, amid all the end-of-day madness, I spotted her walking towards me. I swear it was like a movie. All the other kids were scurrying to hand in finished assignments, pack their bookbags, and grab their coats or jackets, etc. Yet, all I saw was her, approaching in slow motion. Her eyes were glazed as she tossed her long dark hair to the side, holding my letter in her hand. Suddenly, I realized those were tears in her eyes. As if yesterday, I remember thinking, this isn't good, you beyond blew it . . . the poem is so bad you made the poor girl cry.

TRIBUTE TO A WOMAN

xxi

My fragile ego was on high alert. I was already preemptively thinking of something superficial and dismissive to say, along the lines of, "I wasn't even really trying when I wrote it." Anything to lessen the forthcoming blow. However, before uttering a single word, she hugged me, tightly, and was full-out crying. I slowly realized those were tears of happiness. That revelation eclipsed anything between myself and the fairer sex, to that point.

When she explained how sweet and thoughtful, how genuine and poetic my words were, how warm and beloved they made her feel, I was astounded. Something I wrote had such an impact on another person, to the extent it moved them to tears. It was like a veil lifting from my young eyes. I could tangibly see the power of purity stemming from true artistry.

Now, full disclosure, I'll be the first to admit, Langston Hughes, Frost, Keats, Lord Byron, and so on, I, nor this particular poem, was not. I forget all it entailed, but I'm certain it was full of clichés, (smh). It's also highly likely a line or few was "borrowed" from whatever R&B love song I was heavily into at the time, (lol).

However, what I realized in that moment, the single most important thing I discerned, was that sentimentality mattered most. Embers of her emotion, ignited by fiery sentiments of my expression, burned twice as bright and twice longer given the extent of certitude, fanning flames of each word addressed to her. She had no idea, but in that moment, she created a monster in me, (It's alive . . . It's alive . . .) in a good way of course!

Fast forward again, I'm now a sophomore at the biggest and best high school in the city of Chicago. A member of this, the captain of that, I was immeasurably more girl-crazy than before. Yet, as you may have guessed, still writing regularly. Journaling daily in fact, I made incredible strides. I found the tenor of my own voice as a wordsmith, and honed a unique writing style, especially pertaining to poetry.

By then, my confidence was borderline cockiness. I went out of my way to let the world know I wrote poetry. Fear of ridicule was nonexistent. A few years prior, I saw firsthand the scope of my reach. From then after, you couldn't tell me I wasn't the best thing since . . . (feel free to insert your favorite idiom here, lol.) I wrote letters to every girl I liked. Best of all, they were equally well received. Eventually, I took it a giant step further. In full out Cyrano mode, I wrote poems for my closest friends, to pass off as their own, to the various girls they obsessed over. Their positive results further proved I had something special.

That same year, fortunate beyond belief, I became exclusively involved with the greatest gain, the greatest loss of my life. Her untimely passing paralyzed me in so many ways, on so many levels. Poetry, like my perspective on life at the time, had gravely lost its meaning. Writing as a whole was indefinitely on the backburner. It wasn't until another two years later, my senior year of high school, my passion for writing was reborn. Half reluctant, I decided to take creative writing as an elective that year. It turned out to be one of the best decisions I ever made.

Comprised of so many incredible writers, that class breathed new life into my creative spirit, and competitive nature. Our individual letter grades were merited only after every assignment was read aloud, subjected to the earnest critique of the entire class. The nature of this activity ushered me hurriedly from my comfort zone, challenging me to remain consistently on my A-game. It also forced me to develop comfortability, both in sharing my work and in receiving constructive criticism, as equally as praise.

TRIBUTE TO A WOMAN

One student in particular, a fellow named Dominichi, was an exceptional poet. Therefore, I felt compelled to keep pace with him, never one to be outdone. I made a concerted effort to step my game up all the more. I spent many nights well beyond a reasonable student's bedtime, some sleepless, all to ensure whatever I brought to class the following day, was overwhelmingly received. That competitiveness, and all-night writing process, habitually persists to this day.

Compiling our final creative writing assignment, a compilation consisting of our best work throughout the year, in addition to 25 pages of new material of our choosing, was when I first decided, at some point in life, I wanted to eventually author a book. Toward this, my creative writing teacher, Mrs. Barliant, shared some great advice.

I previously expressed to her, my goal was to write on a much deeper, more meaningful level, one that would impact people in such a way, they'd remember me forever. She explained, in order to do so, I would need patience, discipline, practice, and most of all, allowance of time to live. Her reasoning was, the more life experience I gained, the better equipped I'd be in using everything undergone, as a means of more substantive creative expression.

And so, I've lived my life accordingly. I've allowed myself to embrace everything life has to offer, taking the lessons of all my experiences and using them as fuel to constantly reach new heights, to breach new borders as an artist, actor and author alike.

One of the most essential lessons I've learned after all these years is, eventually, memories fade, and most people forget the details of various moments, conversations, and encounters. However, they do always remember if someone leaves a lasting impression upon them, and if so, how they were made to feel in those exact moments.

What's more, the instant my dear friend from seventh grade became moved to tears regarding something I wrote, it became apparent, and pointedly reaffirmed, one life experience after the next, that, what comes forth from a man's heart, truly, purely, and spiritedly well-intentioned, in the same manner, reaches the hearts of others.

On this premise, and as stated afore, truly, purely, and spiritedly well-intentioned, from the bottom of my heart, the subsequent poetry was penned. I hope all I've outpoured within the following pages reaches you all the same!

For every woman infrequently told she means so much . . . .

Tribute to a Woman

My love—
Her place shall be upon pedestals
As petals of roses
Fall freely at her feet,
Undivided and unconditional
Are ways in which she shall garner
This man's attention and love—
My pleasure shall be
Knowing
I am essentially the cause of hers—
What other word but *safely*
Could better describe a way in which
I shall carry her heart,
Just as the term *passionate*
Exemplifies a way we'll kiss,
And ideals of the word *together*
Portrays ways we'll maneuver
Ever facing unforeseen setbacks—
After God, and before myself
Entails realms of her existence,
Through my eyes
Amazingly and in awe she shall be seen,
Within my arms
Tenderly intense she shall be held—
Her every endeavor
Shall be afforded my full support
As well as encouragement,

Any criticism
Shall be tactful
And constructively conveyed,
As we constantly
Challenge one another
To be our best selves—
Doubt and indecision
Are unavoidable aspects of life
So naturally
There will be moments
When an urge to second-guess
Causes her to question
Many choices she has made—
Knowing this
I shall make it so
She has one less worry,
As there will never be a need
To reconsider authenticity
Of what I say I feel for her—
My actions shall serve as evidence—
Of this, men will bear witness
As we first develop
And secondly sustain
Something so special—
Our effort,
Vast majorities shall applaud
While envy of a few remains unmasked—
But such is life, and at the end of days
When our present becomes future's history
Every tongue shall confess—
Truly ours was one for the ages

COREY LEIGH

Evening Gown

I stare long, flowing fabric of her dark-skinned tone
Of thresholds which divide sunny days from starry nights
Measured precise—
Her firmament sown, a singular stitch at a time
Daylight bids a farewell,
Enviable curves clothed in clouds of darkness are stairwells
Her mystery ascending—
Moonlit angles cascade, shimmering
Decoratively arrayed, precious gemstones glinting
Neon crescents incandescent, galaxies gleam in her eyes
Energy explodes—
Layering grounds of my delight in singular stride
Spotlight of her split, cueing dark-chocolatey thighs
Malnourished eyes of mine more heartily feast upon
Her essence, her aura, mannerisms, her mystique
Dual capacity her appeal, she saunters in seamlessly
Scarlett carpets are sheet music, her loveliness a lullaby
Donning gowns of evening's elements—
Her night-fallen melanin personifies a goodnight
Well-dressed in evening's elegance she beams—

Rendering certain souls restless, coaxing others into dream

TRIBUTE TO A WOMAN

A Chi-City Love Song

Whether adverse temperatures or atypical Chicago winters
We were inelegantly known to "Skate on State"
Reservations for two, customary River North dinners
Under ashen moons, overlooking cityscapes

Aside the Daley Center, sensing déjà vu
Flashbacks uncoil, ribbons of fondness are riveted
Recollecting a photo shoot, we two were privy to
Beside Picasso's steel abstract, some time ago visited

Shedd Aquarium Sundays, glass housing translucent fish
Against which, we coined silly faces,
Planetarium fun dates, rousing corpulent lips
As if stitched, we conjoined kissy faces

Millennium Park concerts (symphonic, soul, rock, jazz)
Vocal prowess of various artists, horns of brass blared
Smells of summer blades glowing green, manicured grass
Calls to mind a picnic or few, there amongst friends, we shared

Springtime, sub and/or elevated ("L") train rides
Chicago's Transit Authority, our very own canvas—
Hues of orange and green, red, brown, blue, and pink lines
Brushless, yet out and about, coloring our city romantic

COREY LEIGH

Harlem Nights

Meticulously—
Trained hands of erotic kisses
Hot oil massage body of her apprehension
Chic eyes signify she's on verge of allowing entrance
Willful submission as we submerge
Alas, first and final compositions converge
Penned ink of newfound oneness, whereby
New beginnings are beautifully written—
      Steep thighs, lips laboriously mountain climb
Centerpiece of her paradise, extraordinarily wondrous
Holy ground, new religion
Deep sighs dignify her decision
Jewels of elation, satisfactorily unearthed
Poetic exhibition, my penmanship upon her page
Scribbling, *A Love Supreme* (*A Love Supreme*)—
Brass horns score the rhythm, thunderously
      Her sweet and savory summer rains

TRIBUTE TO A WOMAN

5

Once Upon a Picnic in Central Park

Plaid blankets poured over green blades—
Yellow sundress and white wedges
Impeccably cater to your shape
Cool breeze of our embrace
Coconut-oil-scented neckline
Sense of smell serenades
Freshly, tighter I squeeze
Your melanin sweet and brimming over
Flashless I picture, your body a pitcher
Mouthwatering, chocolate lemonade—
Occupying all streets adjoining my spine
Frost-colored fingertips at present parade
Sparkly red lips—
MAC Retro Matte, Ruby Woo glitter infused,
Unknowingly mimic
Romantic beverages, Laurent-Perrier
Rose´ infused sangria, in which
Rasp, straw, black, and blue— mixed berries bathe
Each plenteous sweet, yet liable to intoxicate—
Crayola of your kisses, unspoken French comprehension,
Etch beyond lines of physical senses
Light-headed as we unlatch, I a lush
In full blush glittering giddily—
Dually, sporting your now smeared colorway

Daddy's Girl

Heiress of the ever-living God—
Jewels of wisdom encrust bezel of your speech
Pillar of strength you are
Akin to rivers of renaissance past, (which were)
Poured of Langston's pen,
Your soul, too, has grown deep—
Royal garbs of virtue
Exceedingly well you wear, redefining chic
An onlooker, I admire
How seamlessly you maneuver
(Even amidst grandest of life's challenges)
Restless waters of fear, doubt, and unbelief—
Undeterred, you reach lighthouse of your dreams
Winds of faith propelling sails, your vessel
Kisses incredibly shorelines of manifest destiny
Inherently, my heart applauds
Appearance of your presence
Gracing critical stages of my life—
Through love's looking glass I am peering
And of endings, in sight none are appearing
Only opportunities for growth
Continuously together
Ultimately surpassing—

Heaven's own heights

TRIBUTE TO A WOMAN

7

Rainbows of Retrospect

Overhead projections—
Rainbows bursting all about
Iridescent color schemes of love
On earth, as it is in heaven,
Are leaves of autumn trees
Falling, diving board for branches—
Persuasive red candor, romance rouses crowds of wanting
Tongues of yellowy-orange flames kiss heatedly
Defrosting frigid mouths of longing
Green fields of infatuation, mutually instep strolling
Aloud, indigo-blue skies cry joyfully
Wateringly nourishing unquenched whims
Softly crushed, beneath bodies of our determination
Violet and lilac blooms cushioning, all the while
Puddles of affection overflow private thoughts
We each splash in smiles of the other—
Shallow blushes cover deep emotion
Each layer peeled away in length of a tryst
Alas, gates to her kingdom are drawn
Upon entrance, two become one and permissibly
A citizen of love dwells royally within her womb—
Her womanly figure externally illumined
Inner prisms reproductively winding lights of new life

Rosie Precipitation

Withdrawn of straw woven baskets—
Their descension an extension of the Heavens
Surfing gradually, foaming waves of gravity
Rose petals rain down delicately
Decorating deeply her dually rooted Afro-Latin frame—
Crimson reds, cotton whites, and flamingo pinks,
Each to her form adhering heavily, drizzling velvety
Contrasting against her skin, so goldenly brown
She lies gorgeously nude
Thornless in bloom
As if she grew from the ground—
Petals puddling bed sheets
Downpour progressively, begetting
Such a sexy, fun-filled atmosphere,
We reel around in revelry
Excitement of enticement, weighted down
One to another, lungs of longing drown—
Whelmed-overly
Upon flowerbed of her precipitation—
Forever Rosalie

(And as an aside)

Jimmied locks to Pandora's box
A pastime paradox, unsealed
Frequently revisiting fleeting memories
Exclusively we used to be
In contradiction simultaneously,
Held in high regard, yet, elusively
Infinitely reminiscing of the one I am missing

TRIBUTE TO A WOMAN

9

Preludes of a Redbone Rhapsody

Once or thrice upon a sweet smelling, naturally long—
Curly-haired, southernly hospitable, slim-thick redbone—
To heaven, those thighs were built like stairways
Upon which, my lips, would eagerly escalate,
In so doing, open invitations obtained
A sweet semblance, similar to Maxwell's *Urban Hang*
Whenever, wherever, while careful not to exclude
Whatever the etcetera, all I know is, if ever
It so happened I were summoned to taste,
Milk and honey of her . . . indeed, I'd partake—
Boldly, as though the tongue were remote controlling
I turned her on, I turned her up
Were pleasure a cliff, we scaled utmost edges,
Tiptoeing ledges, toyed playfully
Precipice of enough enjoyed safely, yet
Seductively pulling back just a little
Building blocks of anticipation, not quite yet time to topple
Classroom of her bedroom
We spelled excitement a bit differently—
Some days it was rough and some nights it was gingerly
Either way, limbs overlapped in pools of intensity
See, my propensity's to please
I trekked milkiest of ways just to get her there

COREY LEIGH

Asgardian to galaxies of her gratification—
All hail princess imperial,
Newly crowned, queen upon a throne of satisfaction
Yes, each stroke sat her there, royally enacted
Now everyone everywhere, all at once, hurriedly hush (shhh!)—
Finally, she's sleeping

Pictured Perfectly
(Inspired by L. Evans)

Wondrously—
Her unveiled body
Speaks thunderously
Of such, godlike artistry
Trumpeting triumphantly, as
Heaven's hue, honey-coated mahogany
Accentuates flawlessly
Every sliver, her well-formed frame—
Flashbulbs are bursting
Deeply intense, kisses commence
Luminous lips of shadow and light
Press sweetly upon each pose, she strikes
Fancifully
Landscape of imagination and fantasy
Her portfolio overflows—
Exquisite calligraphy
Inked in digital imagery
Photographic fairytales unfold
All that *sexy* ever was, is, and, or will be
Iconic ideology, whispered and heard
In sensual soliloquies
Those curves do tell, curtailed
Yet aptly extolled—
Sequentially
Notions of beauty bloom

As I absorb
Sun of such a sultry gaze
Lovely-eyed girl, almond-shaped
Their allure alone
Assures wanting never wanes
Unable to unfix, betwixt
In awe frozen, upon them peering
Fiercely—
Her prints pierce me—
Entangled in such sensual synergy
Her body and lens are one
Amorously enveloped electricity
Derivative of contoured positioning
Head to toe, utterly aglow
Charring intensity, (prodding propensity)
Thoughts thaw as a result—
Her centerfold searing
Whereas, pontificating gorgeousness
Beholding beauty of her frame
Confectionary songstress
Singing songs to my delight
In unison, her curves I am hearing
Vociferously sweet serenades—
Opus of Her Sex Appeal
Photographically paraphrased
Harmonic melodies of her melanin
Curate quietly sum total of her sexiness
My imagination riotously
Covets fullness of her perfection
Ravishingly

TRIBUTE TO A WOMAN

Funnel clouds touch down
Air of unmatched beauty
Ravaging corridors of my mind
Subconsciously
Every corner unkempt
Collapsed quarters
Safeguard no longer, vain attempts
To conceal every facet of feeling ever felt
Circumstantially improper fully disclosed
Therefore, never mentioned, merely dreamt
I surmise, as camera shutters clamor
(So seductively chic is she)
Depth of her glamour, addictively predisposed
Never-ending breadth, her photos
Exhale tirelessly
Kinesis of actuality
Accountably held, wielding
Pinwheels of sentimentality
Forever spinning, deeply within me
Yielding to her only, desirously hailed—
So far beyond confines of purity
She is Eden's Eve, a radiantly redesigned beauty

Naked

I'll always remember, vividly
Exact moment she disrobed her guard and
Undressed her heart
First time in front of me—
Garments of inhibition grew downwardly
As gravity of my commitment had its way—

    Astoundingly

Existentially Yours

Ever so lovingly
She leans in and whispers,
Decoratively
Her words drape fancifully
Lightly lingering my nearest lobe—
Ever so subtly
Fenty-frosted lips produce shivers
As excitement of enticement
Gradually unfolds—
Soft as mid-spring blush
Petals plucked of long-stemmed roses,
Simultaneously simplistic and complex
An eyeless inquiry peering deeply within me
Rhetorically
A two-part question she poses—
"An eternity from now, she begs,
where and how do you see yourself!?"
No response necessary, yet
Overtaken in an urge of open flame
Fueling the feeling, a need to redress—
Never one to speak without thought
I gather myself and proceed to express
Purposely, placing her palm against my chest
Allowing French fingertips to feel
Intensity of openness
As an honest heart, (once and for all)

COREY LEIGH

Lifelong layered in safeguarding garbs
Readily undresses itself—
As calendar years fall by the thousands
And legions of time
Outlasts the mountains and
God's green earth
Aged far beyond its prime, succumbs
Unrecognizable, outfitted in dearth
An old-new-world, wrinkled in time
In you only, its equal sought, found, and realized
I foresee remnants of spiritual energy, my soul
Truest reflection of my former self
Perpetually seeking, metaphysically speaking,
In motion eternally—

        Until a rest in you, once again I find!

Envy of All Women

Footsteps of fascination
You sashay ostentatious
Catwalk of my mind's eye
Set aflame furiously, (flint of each elongated stride)
As a pose, you strike me
Attention span frozen acutely
Flashbulbs bursting beautifully in sync
Each subsequent snap captured alluringly chic

Spaghetti-strapped-M-slit gown
Curves highly esteemed, held within its hand
Aerial suspension, as though positioned upon pedestals—
Postured perfectly, slightly adjusting your crown
Summoning command of your presence, it lands—
Ever clear pronouncement, you came not to play, but rule

Legs long as open roads, aptly toned linear lines
Pendulum of rhythmic hips temptingly hypnotize
Thighs hide and seek seemingly
Pathways to promised lands crossing over dreamingly

Open-toed Rose Amelie Ankle Wrap Red-Sole Sandals
Luxe heels heighten twofold
My own intrigue plus your frame, each fanciful
Summer solstice, sun of your sultry stare astounds
Domino effect, your penetrating glare
Inwardly, residue of reservation all falls down

Traversed runway of my reality
You alone ruptured riotously
Vain attempts to piece together new normality
Forever fruitless in your wake
In no way could any other thereafter, ever replicate
Upstretched standards of excellence, you effortlessly elevate

Stylish appeal, features, rhythms, and mannerisms
Inner diva, (lofty air you exude), in awe, masses mimic
Equal parts confidence and competence, unapologetic
Fierce pursuit of your passions and ambitions, limitless

Strength of your intelligence, your soul supreme, majestic
Anchoring outward vessel of unrivaled aesthetics
Goddess stature, evident magic from inception to finality—
A mysterious magnetism all attempt to imitate, rather inadequately

TRIBUTE TO A WOMAN

Continental Beauty Queen

Beautiful girl—
Skin dark as sides of moons unseen
Majestic and serene, your melanin sheens
Heaven's twinkle tinting shade of your eyes
Planets of possibility, my hopes, and dreams
Orbit uplifting suns of your smile—
In tranquil tarns of your persona I bathe
Aching limbs of frustration and stress
Each wade, soothed in pools of your poise

So full of life you are, can't help but feel
Reborn, newly enhanced, each waking by your side
A regular witness
I've seen you inhale tribulation
Only to, exhale confident faith,
No effort necessary exhibiting dexterity of discernment—
Even in faces of those who deride our bond

Over small talk and envious tongues you tower
An arsenal of wisdom, and love, piercing those opposing
Beneath breast of your chest
Beats a heart at rest upon palms of Midas
Purest of them all—
Admittedly smitten, diagnosed love-stricken
Feverishly fathoming romantic heights
Starry-eyed, temperature of our commitment
Heavenward, breaching cloudless climes

Lovingly esteemed—
Preeminently you hold me, slender yet uplifting arms
Trouble-free you manage to
Haul away prior baggage,
Slates wiped unconditionally clean
Safeguarded in comfort of your embrace

Love, you are my true story
Foundation inspiration was established upon
When it comes to what you do for me . . .
(Heaven only knows)
Couldn't sing your praises
Had I employed a thousand tongues—
Nor pen of your greatness
Had I enclosed a thousand poems

TRIBUTE TO A WOMAN

Revelation

It was a future at first sight—
In you, I saw a queen
Strong enough to lead, yet
Wise enough to know when (and whom) to follow—
True definition of a friend
To be loved, trusted, respected
Counted on, either as favor smiles
Or misfortune frowns, in the face of our bond—
You were dressed in inspiration
Accessorized in support of your man
Fragrance of God sprinkled upon your person,
A heart so hid in Him
Luckily for me, He and I are on the same page—
More than a mother to be, see
You and I soon seated at heads
Of royal generations to come—
At some point, seasons of life
Will prompt change in coloration
Like leaves, upon hairs of our heads
However, looking back I'll be able to say
I lived what was seen at first glance—
Strong and wise enough to lead
Likewise knowing, when and whom to follow
True definition of a friend, (an ending predating its beginning)
You were meant especially for me, my queen—

        Together we'll grow, more than merely old

Baptism

Inhalation held
Crown of my existence, she dipped—
Second time around, alive
Righteously withdrawn from waters of her joyfulness—
Hence, life seen in new light
Dark ages of fraudulent former flames
Singed in beacons of happiness she brings
Furthermore, fully expunged from pages of memory
Emblematically, handmade raiment of love encompassing
My heart, once exposed, no longer naked—
Spiritually, her sustenance draws lines that see,
Dots of my tattered soul reconnected
Prodigally, return flight, back in fold of our Father's grace
Opinionated, we share points of views,
Vastly varying subjects, numbered in multitudes
Ranging wide as widths of infinite—
Verbal volleys fill flowerpots of ideas
Each the better, petals of our person's bloom
Watered in intelligent conversation
I'm so thankful
She took time to learn (both of and from) me
And rather than of myself coax me to give—
She thought it best to earn me
And so, combination of due time and patience
Cemented our bond, most certainly

A Whole New Whirl

Romantic whirl
A wind, which carries
Cool breath of your heart's kiss
Taste and texture are voluptuous lips
Pressed upon centerpiece of mine—
Fondness unfolds
I find myself smothered in awe as
Comprehension of how you feel
Blows me away—
Your glance dawns on me
Warm as summer sun
Upon flowery cheeks of roses
Reddened in blushes of spring—
Sparkle of your smile
Endless span, its glimmer a guide
Points a wayward heart in right direction
Home, having found your side
My once wandering nature
Sees its shoes removed, relaxed
In warmth of your smiles dwelling place—
The more time I spend with you
The more it seems you splinter
Drawbridge of learned defense mechanisms
I find myself falling, oceanic charm
Its waters washing over me
Christened in a pool of your personality's cool—

Snowflakes of your affection fall feathery
Accumulation covers earth of me in entirety
Painting grounds of my delight
Icicle bright, upon slopes of trustworthy
First, our commitment came to crystallize—
I celebrate, nativity of your patience
From day one it was there, never wavered
As occasionally you labored
Pains my stubborn pride did yield
And now, understanding and compromise
No longer underlie
Seed of your influence sown, fully grown,
We reap the ability to tread common ground more easily—
It pleases me, you are someone I look up to, unabashedly
Coupled with ways in which you watch over me
I hereby hail you, my Sky, befittingly—
(Did you know) on lazy days I lie
Alone in fields of dream
Mind occupied in bountiful clouds of your persona,
I insinuate, based on their varied sizes and shapes
Outlined in your likeness, labeling resonates—
Noticing first, huge mountainous puffs
Taking shape of *encouragement* while passing by
Alongside, I see trees of *belief*, sturdy as yours is in me
Clusters of bright-winged birds, in small patches appear
Flown one atop the other
Reminiscent of how, on wings of your love
I am hoisted higher, more so than all others—
Cumulus entities, soft as cotton seemingly, of a sudden
Several merge as one and call to mind *substance*

TRIBUTE TO A WOMAN

Of which you fill my days, to the point of bursting
Images of flowerpots and water pails present themselves
Reflections of times, in humidity of companionship
I wilted nearly, a love-life too long left thirsting
That is, 'til you came along
Showers of your fullness soaked the seed, whereby
Roots of our relationship grew strong—
I awake to find reality
Far sweeter than dream
So much so, wisdom teeth of actuality
Inherently acquired cavities
Reinforced, romance sealed hollowed spaces
As your love filled my heart's hallowed places,
So seemingly surreal, yet here and now I am yours,
Deservedly unreservedly, to you I yield
Incessant end of sweet surrender—

        Whisked away, enraptured in your whirlwind

In Realms of the Sensual

Searing hands of candlelight
Caress delicately our bedroom's body
Draped in dimness, every corner clothed afore
Now stands fittingly undone, stripped
Of its shadowy attire
Remainder of evening retires
Gowns of darkness
Fingertips of flicker loosens and removes—
Crest to lowermost
      Four walls gleam, glitteringly aglow

Honeysuckle sings
Masterfully in four-part harmony
Your spirited scent serenades the senses
Echoes of aroma
Linger long, sweetly amplified
Each note scaled in meter
Of a fragrance so resoundingly pleasing
Desire taps to its tune, meanwhile
Voice of your rhythmically riveting perfume
      Sees lust swoon as it sexily croons

Diamond-like, smiles identical faces of
France's finest sparkling wine—
Twin flutes of its fluidity
Belly dances within our glasses
During intermissions of flirtatious conversation

Laughter-filled pauses, where we
Retrieve . . . sip . . . set aside of a sudden . . .
Only to, eventually latch hold again—
Taste buds applaud
Such a seductive performance,
      Ovations of our intoxication derived

Ten works of art
Purple fingertips drip imaginatively upon
Construction paper of my person
Neck, shoulder blades, and back
Each appear finger painted as you sensuously relax
Natural aromatic oil aided—
Calculus of strenuous tension easily solved
Residue of accumulated stress, remnants of ache
Manufactured in length of laborious days
      Subside lacking trace, thoroughly dissolved

Instantaneous, immediacy of our embrace
Brought about as platoons of pink-truffle kisses
Invade, occupy, and encamp erogenous space
Coloring expertly inside the lines
Nape of my neck to lobes leading
Blisteringly overtaken, bonfire of our lips meeting,
Slow roasted arousal perfectly seasoned
Splashes of our moans covering evenly
Marinated in foreplay, one another well served
Robust multicourse, each fiendishly feasting
Catered plates of ourselves scraped
      Lustful atmosphere of evening

Hearts of those guilt-ridden or grieving
Idioms doubling as depictions only
Portraying nature of our breathing—
Intuitively, as one enlivens pace
Handsomely in step, assuredly the other's keeping
To one another, it's as if
You masquerade as *Dear* and I as *Life*
Way in which we're clinging—
Resigned to till as long as it takes
      As a result, fountains of euphoria springing

Dust of delightful screams, soon settles
Satisfaction, thickly layers shelves of our selves
Ripcords wrenched, parachuting hearts
To normal, their rates return
Fastening our faces upon each other
Pinch of dilated pupils reassures
Something so seemingly unreal, actually was
I catch myself reasoning—
Were this magnificent scene all in my mind only,
In its entirety merely dream
How best would I differentiate reality from make-believe?
Were that the case, I surmise it best to pray—
      (Doubly negative) I never not sleep

An Affair Unforgettable

Even though you don't belong to me—
Coziness of those thighs, feels like home to me (and, uh . . .)
Every moment you spend gone from me (it's like the . . .)
Loneliest of times, amid misty warmth I long to be

Wonder if he knows, you be out on loan to me—
Nature of our escapades, so wrong but see
This no-holds-barred affair, as felicity's hostage is holding me
Soulfully, siren song of your sex so hot, each note scalding me

Sensuously lit, wooden wicks waxed-warm, dripped heavily
Roman candles of our bodies burn devilishly
Explosive, stricken match of oft fulfilled fantasies
On top, underneath, tossed, turned, mixed-up, repeat
A romantic recipe, (from scratch)
Thoughts of French manicured fingertips rousingly caressing me

While you commute— up, down, side to side so pleasantly
Fast or slow, you put on a show, bedroom pageantry
Sun of your sexuality, I rise, I shine, I arrive effortlessly
Unsure which realm of indulgence I prefer more gradually—

Coal in your fire, charred, wildly overwhelmed, or
Enchanting cool of your climax, ultimately extinguished in . . .
An affair unforgettable

COREY LEIGH

Assembly Required

Underneath blankets of a whisper
She tucks in her request
      (Build it up and make it last, baby . . .)
Beck and call of her petition, honoring said wishes
Willingly work it with finesse
Eroticism's rhythm . . . tempo slow . . .
Purposeful, her behest
Peaks and valleys tongue touched, trembling her torso
All falls down, crumbled beneath my caress
Small of her back to nape of her neck
Twenty-four kisses climb acutely,
Tiptoeing crystal stairs of her vertebrae—
Tingles reverberate, effusively, toe to crest
Apparatus of the tongue, her pearl pressed upon, ascension
Revved up within the moment, sexy symbolism
Brim of excitement, leisurely filled
Chills overtake, limbs uncontrollably shake
An impromptu praise dance, mischievous mysticism
Ebb and flow of pleasure, I man the helm
Furnishing as I see fit, withholder in the same realm
Architectural lover, assembly required production
Tore down walls while building up momentum
Her overflow, no longer under construction
High rise of her climax finalized per instruction—
Grand opening, scarlet-ribbon-cutting ceremony
Groundbreaking to breathtaking—

       Bluest eyes of cloudless skies her sighs scrapping

Eclipsed in a Kiss

Beneath silver beams of beauty
Moonlit kisses carousel
(Ever so merrily)
Round and round
My mummified mind
Wrapped in remembrance
Thoughts of you parallel
(Accentuating verily)
Wardrobe of recollection
Reminiscent, acutely akin to
Freshly pruned petals
Prettily pinned upon lapels

Sentiments You Elicit

Your beautiful brown eyes
Light the skyline of my life—
A single glance
And every safety net
Assembled to ensure
This heart of mine security
Becomes needless and undone—
Imagine effects of your gaze

Somehow
Helping hand of your smile
Carries
Ever so caringly
All pangs of my past away—
Refreshingly reassuring
Especially
During days when
Discouragement sees me as prey

From time to time
I hunger for affection—
Luckily
Having never to suffer lack too long—
I grow full quite frankly
As your kiss, touch, warm embrace
(Flourishingly nourishing)—
Each untiringly
Spoon-feeds the soul

TRIBUTE TO A WOMAN

Bevy
(Inspired by T. Barnes)

Leopard print dress—
So well worn, as though a Christmas gift
Spectacularly
Those curves appear packaged in—
In a dreamlike gaze
I stare long at an assortment of sunlit rays,
Golden accessories
Matching her equally glowing skin—
Sparkling smile
Lighting landscape of my thoughts
As soon as right words were seemingly found
I peered into vastness, her beautiful browns—
Lovely eyes
Upon which every single sentiment
Corralled to convey accurately
Sum total of her sexiness
Of a sudden,
All adjectives escaped me—
Left with a sense of restlessness, I sat,
An entire night's long nearly,
Wrestling with an inkling,
To layer her body in kisses so passionately felt,
And all to myself, keep her closely held
For a lifetime—

Never once relinquishing

Cherry Red

Lips encrusted
Cherry colored
Red as the rockets glare—
Upon porch of my mind
Sway thoughts of them
Back-and-forth for days long
Mental rocking chair—
Return me to those moments
Wandered desert of wanting
Your kiss came, flashes
Flooding landscape of lonely—
If only, (for an instant)
I were to, relive such relief
Instead, stuck, snared in recollections
Face of heart frozen
Turned to stone amid memories' stare—
Taste and texture of your kiss
No sooner than recalled, burst into thin air,
Imagination's atmosphere,
Leaving hopes and dreams
In ash covered, sorrowfully smothered—
All the while, remembering what once was
Eternally lamenting how
Even the most cherished, multihued memories
Fade to black and end up eventually
In the Crayola of time—

Indistinguishably discolored

Mental Treasure

In silky-white gloves
Fittingly affixed
Subtle hands
Of southward winds
Brush-back bangs,
Of chimes which hang,
Dangling, afore the face of night—
Springing forth
Born of beauty, such musical delight
Thoughts of you are jewelry-box ballerinas
Dancing elegantly—
Pirouettes of picturesque memories
(Our most precious moments together)
Safeguarded sentimentally
Vault of my mind, you securely reside
Treasured forever, irreplaceably enshrined

November 3rd
(Inspired by B. Horton)

To a woman whose heart was forged in purity
More golden than ancient Egyptian treasure cities
Whom with each new age, her beauty abounds—
Countless displays of selfless interactions
Of each new day, starlight of your compassion
Continuously astounds—
From rising of the sun to setting of the same,
Chorus of my heart choirs aloud your praise—
This being your day my love, I pray at your feet you find laid
The whole of your heart's desires, each bountifully arrayed

Anxiously Awaiting

Alone,
Forget you ever were
His backup plan,
That's why I put you first
He didn't lift you up,
I won't let you down
He was great at giving up,
Incapable of settling down—
You deserve a man with whom
Love, affection, and protection abounds,
Upon which, allow me to expound . . .

Soon—
I see us in all white
A heart once drowsy
Newly risen, livelier in your light
All I have . . . all I am
All I do . . . all I've dreamt
All I want . . . all I need—
You are that and then some
My seven's L, we fit so well, indeed
No longer awkward alone
Better half squared away—
There are no words
Unidentified diction
Impossible to piece together
An adequate depiction

COREY LEIGH

Of what I truly feel . . .
Of what you truly mean . . .
Of what we've come to share . . .
Of all that you bring,
To a once cluttered table
Otherwise known as my life—
Distance between altar and aisle
Shorten with each stride
In turn, with each breath
Anticipation heightens
Nervous? A little . . .
Ready? Yes . . .
Right decision? My life's best,
Easily—
Your dad now leaves you here with me
In rows, upon pews, people are planted
Our parents, by this point
Could be mistaken for willows
As well as your bridesmaids, (each expected)
Surprisingly, so to my best fellow . . .
Lol, big softy! —
It gets awfully
Quiet, moments just before
Vows are to be exchanged
Squeezing my hand as you spar with tears
Your voice cracks
And with that, I cave—
Best they can, umbrellas of our eyelashes
Restrain streams of our lids, unsuccessfully ultimately—
How mommy made daddy cry . . .
An impending story for our offspring forthcoming

TRIBUTE TO A WOMAN

Never Leave

Never leave—
(Baby please, don't go . . .)
In unison we breathe
Closer than praying hands
My lady, forever say you'll be—

    Me, equally as long, your man

When Poems Cry

As I sit here all alone,
Attempting to pen you a song,
Something so persuasive—
Somber tears are puddling pages
An oft overly analytical mind, mired
Amid thoughts muddled in anguish, rationale blooms
Strangulated, increasingly difficult to disclose
I suppose I've gotten what I deserve
Guilty verdict rendered
Found in possession of *some nerve*
To think continuously, I could take you for granted
And of all things, get away with it, humph . . .
As if consequences were incomprehensible—
Heaven only knows how harshly lands realization's lash
Should not have taken you leaving
For me to find meaning in appraisal of your presence,
Immeasurable afore, now no longer present
Away, cloudy err of my mistakes you've flown
Abundance of joy which you were, unendingly gone—
Had I only outfitted you, prior to, more properly,
Kept you clad, cozy wardrobe of demonstrated adoration
Perhaps you'd still be here ameliorating me
Instead, beneath shadeless trees of seclusion, I am sitting
          . . . futilely alone—
Attempting nonetheless to pen *you* songs
Something so persuasive—
Succeeding only in soaking loose-leaf pages

      Drowning words before they're fully formed

TRIBUTE TO A WOMAN

Elevated Frequency

Frequency of her femininity
I tend to tune in, frequently
An alto I presume
Soulful eyes choir thrillingly—
From first words to fluency,
Language of her love, I learned prudently
Sum of a singular glare she affords residually
A feeling as warm as
Strobe lights of summer sun
One thousand days positioned upon
Fields of dream, rich-soil-nursed seed
Gardens of endless possibility bulb—
Invoking images of golden rays and silvery beams
Her smile promptly sparking,
A choreographed tribal dance in comparison,
Sparkling sharply upon river beds of ancient waters
Whereby, queens of Mother Kemet once swanned in style
Majestic hues resonating liquidity's gleam
Wrought serene in reverence, great Euphrates and Nile—
Alive as limbs of lightening
Her pearly touch leaves me struck
Her ever-loving heart and reassuring arms are
Harp strings and angel's wings enfolding
Each time it's me she's holding
All praise to the author and finisher of our faith—
Not only for, in His image and likeness, constructing me
But, having heavenly foresight to in turn, (out of, and for me)
Additionally engineer one as invaluable as she

COREY LEIGH

Reddest Rose
(Inspired by C. Bush)

Red as the *Rose of Sharon*
Preordained, those lips are preludes of Heaven
Gateway to greater dimensions
Purposeful, sent with the intention
I may have life, greater levels of richness
Baptized in such syrupy sweet tenderness
Anxiously— I await return of your kisses

Bows of rain color skies of mind reminiscent,
Recalling glory of your sensuousness
Scripting stories of miraculous matte finishes
Every kiss recounted, most recent to earliest
Memories usher me backward through time
Testimonial rewind, in my head reread—
Like, from Revelation to Genesis

In REMembrance

In dreams of mine
She can be seen, continuously
Faithfully so
Even as
Midpoints discover days
And tardy suns
Allow lingering of nightfall

At peace am I
Occurrences curtains draping
Windows to the soul
Remain undrawn
For I have found
Sealed lids
Reflect her beauty best

Wide-eyed reality
Rendering cause for concern
Witnessing silently
Dark ink of her addiction
(Subsequent manifold afflictions)
Disfiguring completely
Her once colorful canvas

Devoid vibrancy
Masterpiece to lifelessly—
Created by the brush of God, (in the begin)
Yet, ending most unrecognizably

COREY LEIGH

Her Eyes Speak (A Soldier's Story)
(Dedicated to wives of servicemen everywhere)

Her eyes speak—
On verge of teary swells
Narrating tales
      Of how much she misses me
How from time to time
She would watch as
Her own sleep heavy lids shut, and
Imagine that she kissed me
Absent regret
Same heavenly breath
As though first and last were one
Deep, she pressed upon
Taste tattooing my mind
Her intent, that no matter what
This moment I'd never forget

Her eyes speak—
On verge of teary swells
Narrating tales
      Of nights she would kneel
Devoid a single signature
Yet, petitioning thrones of grace
On my behalf
Presence of Christ conversing
Urging He
Shrink-wrap me in His loving arms

Shielding from hurt, harm,
Danger even—
Lone piece, returned to her,
In due season
Cords of her faith occupy
Sockets of spiritual space, interceding
Hinged on her amen, doors to my defense
Swing open, safeguarding power of her prayers

Her eyes speak—
On verge of teary swells
Narrating tales
        Of my face plastered
Photogenic walls of her bedroom
Coated in my likeness
Those frozen moments
Cube cup of her memory
Frosted in fondness and admiration
Despite mercurial growth spurts
Temperatures of my truancy,
Her calm grew tall, supplanting
Triple digits of alone, notwithstanding
Silvery wares, setting tables of time

Her eyes speak—
On verge of teary swells
Narrating tales
        Of trepidation
Split-second revealed
Face of hesitation
Tantamount of disbelief

As though physical company, my
Long-awaited homecoming
Were a taunting dream—
Flown, amid skies of my ears
Kite of her screams
Echoes which were electric
Attached key of her hopes
Lit, as bolts of realization reaffirm
Authenticity of my long-awaited arrival

Her eyes speak—
On verge of teary swells
Narrating tales
                Of an embrace
So long overdue
Accumulated interest, ascertained
Balance of her hug and kiss
Tipped scales of my emotion
Myself, found peering
Weight of her watery gaze
Sees dam of my restraint
Collapse
Colossal floods, my face mirroring hers
Slivers of silence
One another, we hold
Omitting words
And yet—
Clearly, her eyes speak . . .

                Tearily telling tales of how dearly she missed me

TRIBUTE TO A WOMAN

Cia's Ark
(Inspired by M. Gordon)

Amid the Ark of your smile
All my cares are carried away,
Warm as sparkling rain
Those dimples flash
Flooding all sense of fascination—
Persona of my thoughts, stowed away
Vain attempts to conceal
Immense measures of adoration
Unmistakable as mannerisms reveal
Towering regard, for you held—
All the more obvious made
As each interaction
Foreshadows abstraction
Seeing that, more time we spend
More my feelings
Outfitted in restraint, wind up rent—
Ravishingly unraveling a plethora of sentiments

      Previously shrouded in secrecy

Of a Night in Neptune
(Inspired by A. Andry)

Your recent photos
Only reaffirm
What's been known since the beginning—
You are absolutely gorgeous
Handmade of our Maker
Such a lovely frame
Hershey's Kisses coated—
Iridescently adorable, skin tone glowing
Cued in spotlight
Of an electric Aussie sun—

Amazed I look upon
A maze, prior thoughts are lost
Gone, one-way ticket
Seated on wings of, *forget it . . .*
Your beauty bearing down on me—
Derails the senses
Locomotive of emotional content
Unstoppable
Like a film with Denzel starring
Reaction you elicit, jarring

Of a night in Neptune
Taken aback
Like desert trees
Your palms planted across my back

Automobile of my body
Parked parallel between sidewalks of your lap
Stage of my lips, kisses of yours danced in tap—
Very day, lingers still
I have but close my eyes and feel
Your body, warm beneath my caress
Ginger root of said occurrence, though sweet
My intent I perceive
May have been lost in translation—
Perhaps I misspoke, microphone of body language

That night was about way more than the sensual
Sleigh of lofty aspirations ultimately were led by
Red nose of sincere curiosity,
Merely wanting to (in totality)
Learn you better, earn scholarship for your lecture
Immersing myself in discovery
Studiously uncovering
All that lies beneath the beauty, (abundantly bestowed)
Up to and including, intellectual,
As well as spiritual sides of yourself—

All this time thereafter, often I have felt
As though I overstepped
Boundaries
That day forward, you seemed to set
Barricades
Keeping me miseducated
A nonparticipant of graduation
Never permitted to declare a major
Unable to ever satisfactorily move forward

COREY LEIGH

Prerequisite of friendship left unmarked
Therefore, no advancement ever obtained
Absent proper foundation,
Capstone of commitment disallowed
Never coming to know any more about you than
Surface-level residue of memories
Leftover from conversations concluded that night

It's been years since
Still, I find myself awkward in your presence
Overly analytical
Always wondering where the breakdown occurred—
What was it exactly which kept us from becoming,
More than mutually attracted acquaintances?
Friendly albeit
Yet, far from actually defined as friends—
In any case, at conclusion of days
I merely hope you know
Yes, I believed you beautifully desirable
As a person foremost
A close second, concerning physical
I truly adored you
More than, if told, you'd even believe
Were sentiments regarding you
Never evenly exchanged
Simply getting to know you better than best,
(Even amidst misfiring)
Was always my utmost aim

TRIBUTE TO A WOMAN

Breadth of Fresh Air

Air of *God* initially
Drove breath into newly formed man—

Poet's pages come to live
Only after breathed upon in pen—

So, too, meeting *You* has meant
Once and for all, alive I am—

Born again breathing *You* in, verily
Breadth of love's verity, widening all the more, invariably

Heart Beneath My Chest

Heart beneath my chest
Speaks as it beats
Ancestral drum
Your name bellowed
Fullness of your femininity
Praises are sung
Ladder of your magnetism
I cleave to its rung
Needle of your favor
I crave being stung
Infectious affection
Predisposed, unmistakably suffering from
Withdrawal, ever situated
In shadow of your absence—
You are easily the
Headline and footnote of my life
In closed-caption
Nonverbal cravings unfurl
Entwined in your rapture
Ways in which you've wooed me
Surpasses wildest of dreams
I can't help, stop, fake, nor off, shake it
Sensuously unrivaled, your
Command cannot be counterfeited
Nor your knack duplicated

Hallways

Dark halls of loneliness—
Your love lit the way
Rapid ascension
Spiraling staircase of commitment
Eagerly climbed (as a result)
Our souls, each glistened—
Luminous lips of companionship
Smeared sweetly, deep kisses
Layered in light, leaving
Cheery, cherry face of our bond

A Cinematic Midtown Manhattan Love Scene

Amidst action fading in—
Riesling corks atop rectangular coffee table
Tilted over, at rest upon their sides
Living room shades lowered still
Veiling the face of an electric sun
Optimistic wine glasses remain
At one's side, stick of your lips lightly pressed upon
A tray made of clay ruined in pentamerous pieces
Its ashes, Indian style seated, amid
Your soft, yet frizzy, cream-colored throw rug
Sectional couch cushions displaced
Articles of clothing
Cover hardwood flooring like outpouring puzzle pieces
Southeast corner of the room,
Undergarments hang glide a ceiling fan
Red-laced stockings and brassiere, warmly jacketing lampshades
Audible static of a songless stereo,
Its two cents added,
Fingerprints tattoo a wall mirror
Situated nearby
In mounds, upon your mantle
Rests wax of once, WoodWick, coastal sunset scented candles
Enough even, to fashion a miniature statue
OMG, what a lovely mess we made
As I arise, epicenter of chaos's gaze
I see you . . . really see you . . .

Peacefully sleeping, face subtly aglow
A while I look on
Comeliness contrasting clutter
An antonym of the confusion
Four walls now stand coated in
Chills parading streets of my spine
Prompting my mind to revisit
Actuality of the moment
I now notice formation of geese
Descending lake of your shoulder blades
And aptly apply more covering,
Quietly, smile etched face and all
Your coffee and breakfast become my cause
I press my way to La Cocina—
Alarm clock of aroma ushering your awakening
Cup and saucer of silence soon shattered
Cherry blossoms of our blushing reignite acquainting
Eyes fastened to one another
Appetites appeased, yet there persists unspoken craving
Pros and cons of midmorning misbehaving, hmm . . .
Each aware the other's weighing
While to black, traces of reservation rapidly fading
Abrupt reengagement, entangled in continuation—
Seamless, tailoring love to our own interpretation
Scissoring red tape of society's sanctimonious restraints—
And away, we cut

COREY LEIGH

Rafting

Absent oars—
Lustful eyes of mine
Unthinkingly submerged,
Dreamingly gleaming
All the way down,
Joyously drowned
            Capsized—

Rowing rivers of her curves

Night and Day

It's nighttime nearly—
Departing ever so dearly
A no longer lively sun
Offering one last sigh
Graveyard of westward sky
Born of dawn, to dusk returned—
Ray was precise—

      Night time's the right time
           To be with the one you love!

Therefore, draw near unto me hurriedly
Separately attached, light of day, disallowed to be
Yet, shadows of night offer opportunities to unlatch,
In unmatched air of each other's company
We romantically reconvene
Inhalation detained during day, of evenings we breathe
Freely engaged, partaking apiece in all we allege
Undeniably alive as lovers . . .

    Even if sinfully

Marvin's Room

As Marvin plays in the background
Bring your body to the forefront—
Sensual devotion, known as foreplay
Similar to storefront churches
Aligned along inner-city avenues—
Designed to set the tone indeed
Hearing your body growl
By spoonfuls, allow my lips to feed
Your appetite for excitement,
Such a lovely frame
Beholding picturesque curves—
Step on out of that dress now girl
Slowly, imitating axis upon which the world turns,
Let those spaghetti straps sink sluggishly
As they near flooring, arousal heightens lustfully
Prelude to promise land of satisfaction
Causing effectually, us to want it all the more—
Intangibly, grip of desire tightens
In its vice, lets lose ourselves
Upon my lobe, downy whispers
Articulating it's all mine
Threadbare, all of it splendor
Tonight renders, ample opportunity to prove
Dual instruments, our bodies produce
Slow and nasty grooves, erotic music
Jubilant as old-school juke joints were known for

TRIBUTE TO A WOMAN

The only holding back, entails you holding on to mine
Mutual intent of ours, to make it last, is a tourniquet
Tying bleeding hands of time
Stretching limits of indulgent adherence
To Dr. Gaye's prescribed *Sexual Healing*
Borderline addiction, ever we get that feeling—
We pour out of ourselves, wholly
Pleasure mounting its own Olympus
All we have is all we've given—
Amorous arms of exhaustion
In its embrace, an exhilarating submission

As We Lay

As we lay—
Our perception of worldliness
Roundabout becomes
Water-colored in remnants of love
Most recently made—
In concert we observe
Drowsy rays, sleep-heavy gaze
Of lukewarm summer sun
Nodding its way away from lines of our sight
Dimly, its head lays upon gently
Fluffy pillows of westward sky—
Out comes lipstick, a silvery light
Withdrawn from glittery handbag of night
Marking out the mouth, an attractive moon
She enters the room
And kisses sweetly day a goodnight

As we lay—
Our legs are laces
Crisscrossed, one to another
Smile etched faces are
Emanating pearly luster
Your bangs brushed aside
Forehead pressed against mine, pasted
Closely cuddled, so lovingly sweet
Pastry of said occurrence— sliced, served, tasted
Practically

TRIBUTE TO A WOMAN

As we lay—
Far East island blue
Waters of your tenderness
My thoughts wade warm, while
Hazel eyes stare back at me
Curators of how much you care
Explanatory, despite lacking speech
Conveying expressively
Regard your heart holds of me
Fireside flames, same shade as tangerines,
Pucker and proceed to kiss, romantically
Each corner of our bedroom
Blanketing, our unclothed selves

As we lay—
Atop book shelves, orchids are onlookers
Perched perfectly, I imagine our actions
Answerable, for deep flush of their cheeks
Petals whitish prior, now appear
Timorously pink
Of a sudden, lids become cumbersome
Tilting scales of sleep
I fret not as darkness brought about
Jeopardizes love's color scheme—
Knowing, morning merely means
Carousel of our continuity, recharged
A chance to love even better than our last
Restarts—

    Even as we lay

In Realms of the Senses

Her body—
Lightly doused in dusts of gold
    A glorious glimmer, I undoubtedly remember
Richly enveloping her figure
    Affixed, atop crowned heights unto her soles

Her voice—
Woven words of silky sound
    Specifically, spun for ears undressed
Fully clad, though it were, in Sunday's best
    Ever my name upon her lips resound

Her fragrance—
No will necessary, hers inherits a room
    Distinctively sweet, inviting as RSVP's
Lasting, long after exits were ceased
    Beneath her dizzying scent, desire shrooms

Her kiss—
Fever pitched, luscious Luxe Matte lips, indubitably
    A flint-birthed flame, a fuel-nursed blaze
Caramelized, daydreams dissolve as they flambe
    Sizzling sweet, taste buds awaken to her cherry jubilee

Her caress—
Needful, neckline to torso gently kneading
    Stage of me, gracefully, her hands do dance
Arabesques of retrospect, I never stood a chance
    Intrinsically propelled, aloft her touch leading

Heavens Licorice

Heavenly, her undressed body
Dipped in dazzling dye
Evening sky, her skin tone equivalent
Starry-eyed, I
Tighten laces of imagination
Stretch limbs of sensual whims
And see them relay vividly
Encircling indoor tracks of my mind
Such a supple frame
Lovely inflection, her coal-colored complexion
Mirroring, selfsame,
Every aspect of nightfall—
Coloring my senses enthralled
Soliloquies of private thought
Incite riots, centered around arousal
Of a season, I spring into action
Prickly, heels of impulse spur me along
As we connect
Clasp of her grasp possesses me
Pins of realization all fall down
As acuity strikes, suddenly
I come to know
How moons must feel, cuddled up to exquisiteness,
Each night beholden to coal-colored skies—
Heavenly ascension
Moon of my manhood beaming
Fully risen amid her richly exquisite
Licorice-like thighs

Coming Too

Lips—
Cotton candy soft
Every kiss is a sugar rush
Spangled nails—
Coffin-acrylic fingertips static cling
Across my back like braille, such an electric touch
Legs—
Long as chorus lines touting time coming
(Lyrically, a Sam Cooke signature song)
Promising and to perfection, aptly toned
Around my waist, wrapped like a present
Anticipation of long-awaited penetration
Passionately epitomized, playing afore
Therefore, savoring every second
Butterscotch skin tone—
What is this, velvet!?
Body heat soaring
Inside, her cloud's pouring
Bedroom hibachi hot, if we keep going
Surely these laundered linen sheets soon to be melted
Her body—
Neither paperback nor hardcover
Only, reading her needs I discover
Summarily overdue
To be loved, to be loved . . .
Oh, what a feeling—

Like America, she's coming too

TRIBUTE TO A WOMAN

Excursions

Entrance upon sacred ground
Grateful for admission
She takes me in, deeply
Spots sought to seek
Lesser men do drown
Loud as the rolling sea
In ripples, pleasure resounds
Parallel flesh, akin to breath of her breast
Raised anchor of apprehension
Adieu, bid shores of unfulfilled dreams
Her exhale sets sail, and
We proceed gingerly—
Anything deemed routine we deviate
Fore, during, and after play
Course of our conquest
Charted extemporaneously
Instinctual inner compass
Comes in handy as I cruise,
Southern tip of her peninsula
Coursing cool warmth, her womanly waters
Previewing, what marvels may come
Breaching beyond borders
Discoursing
Behind confines of closed quarters,
She foremost, then me—

       We arrive as always, in chronological order

Diamond Milk

Made up magnificently
Stained-glass mirroring
Lustrous lips are fingertips, seemingly
Pressed upon pulse of my neck
Beneath pinch of your kiss
Its pace quickened
Functional fault lines rendered
Rousing, manufactured rifts
Trails of Fenty Beauty's Diamond Milk
Sparkles against backdrops of self,
Mine own, deeply pronounced ebony skin—
Stirringly, each lobe to torso your kisses descend
Simultaneously charting and unveiling X's
Subterranean stretches, troves of craving
More aurous than ancient treasures, Mayan or Aztec
Buried within, suddenly, surface protruding
Tremors of tension inducing precious spectrums of euphoria

Touch Screen

Touch screen of my torso
Your fingertips ring my exchange
Dialed away from saccharine dreams
Eyes, soaked in sleep prior, readily answered
Sprung forth lively, sun-dried
Rapt in golden rays, your
Rose-gold silk camisole negligee
Fits as if tailor-made
Wintry wind of the moment
Pinwheel of my heart swirls
Recalling previous moments
Mirroring the current
Where cauldrons of pleasure stewed, in thick of it all
Blood pressure stood, bubbling over
Crowd of speech as I attempt to speak
Your hush falls over
Index finger latching my lips' gateway
Straight away, you proceed to pierce
Ears of excitement showcase shiny jewels of our sighs
Dressing room of our bedroom
You, tried me on for size
Perfect fit, your body I mannishly enveloped
Red room of our bedroom—
Photographs of fulfillment devilishly developed

Birthday Suitable

Ways in which she takes it all off . . . slowly
Signaling me hither . . . boldly
Birthday suit center-folding, goldenly glowing

Marigolds in southern fields, soft breeze blowing
Synonymous of how I feel, as, her I am holding
Desire whirls, we unwound in pools of longing

My name skinny-dipped, whispered waters of her moaning
Ignited embers of an ego, swelled in her stoking
Thrilled waters run deep, in unison stroking

Sandy, beach of satisfaction, mutually reached, foaming
Waves of elation, residually ripple, ebb and flowing
Aftermath thereof, praise of her fame forever extolling

Before. During. After.

Before—
>   Incredible
>   Four syllables of description
>   Summarizing a moment
>   We two first shared—
>   Smothered in awe
>   Almost lost for words
>   Shortness of breath while gathering nerve
>   To extend unto you my hand—
>   Awkward . . .
>   Uncomfortable silence followed
>   As you perused my parameter . . .
>   Ultimately partaking in
>   Exchange of pleasantries, mentioned afore—
>   Sighs of relief rippled on the inside
>   Outwardly, a more confident smile I donned
>   Touch of your hand
>   So delicate, so soft
>   Beauty of your eyes, I recall—
>   Equal to or greater than all intention
>   The word itself [beauty] was
>   Originally invented to portray—
>   Ahead of separate ways, an embrace engaged
>   Reigniting within me
>   A plethora of emotions
>   Extinguished tearfully
>   Leap years before we met

COREY LEIGH

During—
   As faultless air, longingly awaited
   Your love overly fills
   Lungs of my life in its entirety—
   I exhale eagerly in order to
   Receive of you, all the more—
   As we become one
   It's like, we reshape lines which define
   Pure, in newness of one another
   Sacred symbolism,
   Unified shrines of ourselves
   Illumined, we leave frost of lonesome liquefied
   Dancefloors of friction
   Raved, well into the night
   Penless, novel songs of delight
   Written in our rhythm
   Two selves, so wholly given
   Beauty cries upon its entrance
   Birthed of our bedroom
   As you allow me to reside within
   Art Deco accented, interior of your privilege—
   I literally feel as though
   We're reducing distance
   Bridging domains,
   Eighth-light equaling, (of heaven and earth)
   A divide expunged
   As we continuously plunge
   Deeper, newfound realms of rarity—
   True oneness uncovered
   Wondrous revelry of clarity

After—
Archetypes of black angels in flight
On wings of airy kisses
Flame-colored lips of candlelight blowing
Crystalized ceilings
Chandeliers of shadows glowing
Praiseworthy, airways of eroticism
We breathed new life
Greatest elements of she
Alongside all that's best of me
Merged perfectly
Producing a moment so lovingly sweet
In effervescent ink, a syrupy heat
Tattooed our room, full-bodily
Chills of love's humidity humbled me
Upon satin pillowcase of surety
My overanalyzing mind gently laid—
Vocal tones of our actions
Humming hymns of sensual whims, upon
Podium of pillow-topped mattresses,
Pews of impassioned sheets,
Sermons of stimulation spiritedly preached,
Poignantly conveyed—
Pendulum of procreation, each heavily swayed
At present, future professions previously unbeknownst
Destiny manifested, unknowingly until
Immediately *after*, *during* introductions just *before*

COREY LEIGH

Metallic

Heat of hearts
Melting
Metallic love
Welding
Cooled by a kiss
Rinsed in a gaze
Smiles which drench—
Within our own blush we're bathed
Burnished luster of our love
Stainless, still to this day

Crown Jewel

Crown jewel of my life
As your man, all that I am
Adorned in the immense
Magnitude of your influence
A better me, you bring to bear
Effortlessly ushering new air
Lungs of solitude sprung
Alive all at once
Cradled in assurance we share
Something so unbelievably rare
Along love's lifeline
Two souls so entwined
Were one without the other
Consider suns prohibited shine—
Upon face of my heart
Darkness once fashioned deep
I learned, convened in your charge—

> Where there is light, darkness must cease

Fireworks

Sparkling spectacles
Sprinkling
Warmly over silent waters
Firelit skies
Rhythm and blues of each eruption
Spews its own pattern of colors
Leisurely dripping
Down canvases of nightfall—
Foreground of such beauty
We stand adjacently frozen
Wearers of delightful chills
Brought about as results of
Fondness for such moments, we two
Hand-holding, fingers enfolded
Lovingly, yours between mine—
Looking down I notice
Painted nails, perfectly coated
Artistic acrylic, individual designs
Glitteringly dripping against an ebony backdrop,
Dark hue of mine—
As if you yourself were
Firelit (and raining down)
Upon I, your very own canvas (of)—

Night-fallen sky

TRIBUTE TO A WOMAN

Decorated in Her Embrace

Citric lips, of
Lemon-lime rains
Kissing lips, of
Our bedroom's windowpanes
On an empty stomach
Heaven growls,
Thunderous sounds
Shattering patterns of slumber
Forty winks, by this point
In as many pieces—
We arise from under
Cool warmth of smooth covers,
Satin, black-cherry colored, as a result of
Early morning outbursts of summer
Eyes equally red as blushing numbers
Set upon faces of patronizing alarm clocks
Bedside, ours mocks, knowing full well
As tilted scales
Heavy measures of contempt I feel
Bearing burden of their buzzer—
Her quintessential candidate
Nominated and elected, all in one
I earn the right to become entrusted
Unattached from comforts of pillow top cushion,
Charged with shutting of casement shutters
Trudging begrudgingly,

I set myself to task
Temporarily paralyzed as Polaroids of lightning
Unexpectedly flash
Languidly, I saunter back to bed
Arms outstretched, she
Warmheartedly welcomes me in
Oh, comforts of such silky shea-buttered skin,
Around me wrapped, fancifully
Reverting back to dreams, decorated in her embrace—

Luxuriously

Seedtime and Harvest

Her soul, righteous in spirit and truth, rainfalls
Watering soil of my sadness
Withered disposition of contentment
No longer lifeless
Exuberant,
Vines of deportment grow in gladness
Sweltered of solitude, my once wilted attitude
No longer draped in dreary
Proud to proclaim, I bloomed—
Green thumb of her godliness a footstool
Sense of jubilance, she brought to bear
Within me, and caused to heighten—
Lofty, dreams grew from minute to giant—

Loamy soil of her soul,
Rooted in and rained upon, righteously

Strong Tower

Like the Tower of Pisa—
You allow me to lean
In times of need
Greatest to least
On you, your shoulders seem
So broad, bearing burdens—

Both yours and mine alike

Yolanda Parker
(Inspired by & dedicated to Y. Parker)

Given to me as a gift,
Upfront I understood
Forever was not our fate—
Time was of the essence indeed
Coming soon to reacquire you—
No matter how close we became—
Though numbered,
Your days were well served
Watching you fulfill your purpose
Touched tenderly upon my innermost emotions
You, you were a guiding light
Brilliantly burning beginning to end
You, you altered my life
Lovingly, wick of my soul singed in your flame
Never to be extinguished—
Yours is a space where there's no place or time
There, of you, any seeker would assuredly find
Hallmarks of heartfelt impressions
More than merely left behind, rather
Long-lastingly, etched into fabric of my existence,
Though absent in physical form—
For you, I pledge to burn
Twice as bright, knowing—
That, that is what you'd want

I, Apart from Thee

Harmonious laughter
Lends itself lovingly
Filling spaces of a hollow heart
You, teach me unconsciously
And, reach me predominately
In an array of ways
Others never quite knew where
(Nor how) to impart—
As light makes love to dark
And newness is conceived
Birth of your **morning** means
Breath of my **mourning** ceased, and
Alas, cycles of life in love
Fashion themselves complete—
      JOYFUL!
      JOYOUSLY,
      JOYFUL!
Daughter of the ever-living God
I, traipse winding roads of thought, and
Always end up at odds, an
Introspective debate, I
Affirm and oppose in unison how
Best to convey, I
Adore you wholeheartedly, as
Sustenance of your esteem

Engrafts itself enduringly, among
Every single portion of me—
So much so, examining eyes of
Wise, well-learned men
Deem it difficult to differentiate, verily
I— apart from thee

Thresholds

Threshold of new beginnings—
Can hardly wait to carry her
Priority shipped, God's delivering
Promises fulfilled, very moment I marry her
Thoughts alone overflow, so much so
I breaststroke in their sweetness,
Dually attired—
Physically, custom-fitted tuxedo
Spiritually, outfitted in her completeness—
Strength lies beneath
Veiled beauty of her meekness
Anxious patter, capricious patterns
Between prayer . . . scriptures . . . vows . . .
Anticipating pronouncement
My heartbeat speaks, as though thinking aloud
Geared up to be allowed,
I cannot wait to kiss those lips
My one and only love—
Countless ways were paved for you to grow close to me
A graduation of sorts,
Off all fours, beyond stages of infancy
We've crawled and stumbled, walked and ran in love
Now it's time we leap—
As God looks over, family and friends look upon
We seal and cement our bond
An intricate wonder, woven web of our wedlock—
Collectively spun

Song of Celebration

In celebratory song—
You are music to innermost emotional eyes of mine
Monumental heights, Everest high, personify our love life
Atop which, twin souls of our union
Harmonize in unison
To have and behold
Two halves now whole
Matrimonial theme songs jointly composed
Accompanying violins and woodwinds
Roots of our love stemmed of
Chords of one accord, whose eighty-eight keys are petals
Pressed upon beautifully,
Grand branches of ebony and ivory pruning, our
Spiritual, physical, intellectual, and sentimentally sensual,
Pianos are blooming, echoing auditoriums of the ages
Looped long-lastingly, love song of our celebration

In Jeopardy

Occasionally—
Other arms reach out to me
Brazenly—
Other eyes do smile, tenderly
Affronted—
Prizing you above all others
I remain unphased faithfully
Loyally unwilling to risk nor wager
Amassed equity
Accumulated interest of our relationship
In no shape, form, or fashion
No person, place, nor thing, could I ever imagine
Coming between, interrupting, or unraveling
This thing of ours,
Leaving all we've built in jeopardy—
  (In homage to Alex)
What then is destiny?

First Season of Loneliness

Winter—
White as garments of God's only begotten
Seated upon purity, His throne as golden, I imagine
As the very rule righteous men aptly adhere to—
Lauded as the gates themselves
Pearly flakes, distinctly shaped,
Born of ash-colored clouds
Descend unhurriedly, though purposely
Proceeding to decorate
All of which once laid bare
Crystal garbs fit snuggly
Icelandic atmosphere of evening
It tugs at me
As I lay alone, adrift seemingly
Semi-sleeping
Nightmarishly dreaming
Silently screaming, as
Arctic fangs of reality
Restrict veins of normality
Frostbitten limbs of logic and reasoning
Mental amputee
Absent any ability
Unable to comprehend
How it is, you're not here with me—
Chills of realization (of which)
I perspire blisteringly

COREY LEIGH

Encased in frames of frenetic energy
Jolting, its voltage
Casts out and reels in
Of wistful waters, a weary heart awakened
Half-frozen, slivers of sadness accumulate
Glitteringly, mirroring just as distinctly—
Gem-stoned flakes mentioned afore
First snowfall of loneliness
Of this I am sure
Days ahead, I'll undoubtedly dread
Attempting to tread a smothered terrain
Its face frozen blue
Icy grounds of solitude, a slippery slope
Heavily glazed, wintry haze of your truancy
I saunter nimbly and still all underneath me
(An aquatic trail-way of happier days), caves
Weighted down, cinderblocks and chains of angst
An apprehensive heart sinking
Trapped beneath enormity of your disappearance
Glacial, eyes have looked their last
Watery grave of tumultuous tears, their final resting place

In Realms of Remorse

Amid castles and courtyards
Yours is a throne of fondness—
As garments of scarlet carpets
Adorn plentifully, halls, chambers, and passages
Golden as king's and queen's scepters and chalices
Thoughts of you (your persona)
Invade and occupy my emotional palaces
Which house otherwise, only
Royally restless heart of mine
Lonely, awaiting reign of your return
Wishful eyes peer lengthy
Through lenses of memory colored in rose
It appears hindsight harrowingly foretold
Absent proper appreciation
Throne of affinity, you'd vacate eventually
Handful of memories are now all I have left
Their penchant, in comparison pales
Your physical company (far away for far too long)
Unendingly gone
Born as a result of you becoming privy to
An inappropriate affair of unappreciation
Cavalier in carrying on, openly inattentive and self-absorbed
And of your needs, negligently dismissive
Ensnared in an entanglement
My own misguided ambitions a mistress
Offspring of your resentment distastefully beget—
Vain attempts to reconcile, turnstile
Consecutive seasons of regret

COREY LEIGH

Starless Eyes Are Crying

A thousand nights have cried
Futile attempts to wipe starless eyes
Consoling suns stay as long as they can
Yet, once daylight bids good-bye
Nightfall weeps all over again—

Numerous occasions
We danced her away
I recollect even, how
Avidly she fed off feverish love
We were known to create
Pastimes, prayers she assuredly overheard
Arguments even, once in a while endured—
All the while, looking on lovingly, as
Bright beams of light shone in her skies—
Ever since we've parted company
Sadness veils the face of night

Midmost juncture
Of peaceless sleep, torn away
From dreams often I do rise
Perspiration on the rocks
Awakening heartachingly
So loud resounds echoes of sullen cries
Ongoing and alarmingly
Bass drumming inner ear of my
Fragmented emotional gate

Return to me my love—
Serve as periods bringing up the rears
Subsequent to sentences of starless tears
Metaphorical homecoming
Punctuation of your reappearance
Ending unwelcomed long-suffering—
Nightfall, nor I,
Care any longer to experience

One Day, Someday, Soon?

Head hanging down
All day I lay around
Shut up in my room, gasping
Smothered in solitude
Desperate thoughts aim to defraud
Doubting Thomas of my heart, with
Hopes of your return—
One day, someday, soon

I fall to pieces—
All the king's horses and men
Collectively handicapped
Incapable of suturing
A heart once hot air ballooning
Beneath fire of your sweetness
Deflated, reflections resemble incompleteness
Your love no longer looking back at me
Too long immersed in coldness of this calamity
Frost bit dreams of love become
Unpopularly amputated, surgical wares of reality—

Head hanging down
All day laid around
Shut up in my room, gasping
Counting ticks of every clock's tock
Tallying wasted time essentially—
Sentimentally marooned
Aiming to defraud my doubtful heart—
Thou shall return—
One day . . . someday . . . soon?

Quicksand

Watery sands of my mistakes
Sinking
Exactly what was I thinking?
Hollow hands of rhetoric
Sways the rope ringing
Bells of blank expression
Loud speaker my emotional ear
Admittedly
Undeserving of its extension
Branch of your forgiveness
Regardless its intention
Rescued me, from under my ways—
Drowning in error
Foolish indecision
I could say I'll never
Here on out, this, that, the third
Etcetera, etcetera . . .
Only, I'd much rather
Demonstrate the change you need to see—
Allow my actions then to alter
Material of belief, and foster
An ensemble so distinct—
Befitting of your trust all the more, fashionably

Stars in Mason Jars

Achingly—
Pillows pressed over my face
Still so depressed
In seclusion I lay
Free hand of mind
Attempting to retrace
Memories marred
Your absence defaced
Great wall of my heart
Brick and mortar decayed
Away, you've stayed
For your return, so long I've prayed
Gallery of my life once more
Your heart rehanged—
Priceless work of art you are
A romance reconvened
Redecorating darkness
Whereas stars in mason jars
You'd shine just as bright
As lightning bugs or fireflies,
(Geographically speaking)
From backyards or forest preserves,
Signifying summertime,
Our season of love, reestablished—
Recapturing that, I've painstakingly prioritized

Melancholy

When she left, initially, I
Thought it would be light pain—
As it turned out
Inconsolable eyes welled, wetter than
Forty-day-and-night rain
In solitude, shortness of breath sprang
An immeasurable amount of weight came
Crashing down as all around
Structurally deficient walls of realization caved—
Upon landscape of my heart
No trace of a single ray, light could not be found
A soul once fluorescently free
Now hostage, held as darkness abounds
Once a bright flame, second she left,
Dark shadows of death
Our bond became—
Dense fog of foolish pride wouldn't allow me to see
My best friend, there, before my face
And by my side, the entire time, loyally
Now, no matter how fond,
Memories alone won't ever replace
And with that, finality of the moment,
All around me grays to black—
No foreseeable way forward, sightless
Blinded by my own egotistical shortsightedness
Mourning a morning that never came

COREY LEIGH

Oh, What A Way

Lights of love turned down
Heart's door slammed shut
Oh, what a way to be feeling—
The day my baby left

Of a soul sorrowful
Baptized, chilly waters of regret
Oh, what a way to be feeling—
Forgiven for misgivings but she doesn't forget

Perilously restless
Analyzing overly, every argument uttered afore
Oh, what a way to be feeling—
When it comes to rekindling, she isn't sure anymore

Better suited, necessary improvements
Time away wisely spent, (introspectively examined self)
Oh, what a way to be feeling—
Watching her from afar, far happier with someone else

Excalibur

The hardest part
Of having a hardened heart
Is when *the one* comes along, alas
Capable of clearing sword from stone,
You know, remnants of your ex's caliber—
Mustering courage
To unclothe yourself of disbelieving armor,
Strip away imprudent pride and fear
Start vulnerably anew,
Hitching faith to carriage of their intentions—
Simply allowing them to show and prove
Not all lovers seek to misuse and,
Not all fairy tales lack truth

Revamped

Last lover came and went—
Her emotional miscues
Predating barriers
Bordering an awkward heart

Stench of mistrust still lingers—
Unseasoned, tossed to the side
Looked over, left out
So long, it soured

Within her marathon of misuse
Frustration ran rampant
While once smitten, time revealed
Fang of her commitment rabid

Her storm blew the roof
Shook foundations of deep feeling and pride
Nearly leveled mansion of me
Where which this thing called love resides

Sleeves of patience, upwardly rolled
You stepped forward, assumed role
Restoration's ringleader
Right woman you were, makeover specialist

Face of damage beautified,
A self newly restored—
Sole reflection of all your effort
Renewed sense of worth, you alone responsible for

TRIBUTE TO A WOMAN

Ledges

One foot bravely fronts the next
Off ledges of l-o-v-e I stepped,
Bottomless, into her wholeheartedly fell
Hardly, only absent hurt
Oddly, elderly aches
Wrinkled in times of heartbreak
Hordes I never could quite shake
Finally dispersed
No longer occupying
Streets of a more willing heart
In earlier times, somber eyes
On occasion catered cries
Those wells now sealed
Forever dried out
Amid unwavering warmth
A generous joyfulness, exuding her—
Solitary portion of our circumstance
Deemed problematic as
Inductions of each new day spring
More difficult than the prior, whilst
Critically attempting to fathom
Which part of opportunity afforded
I prefer the more—
Arms enfolding her at eventide,
As she drifts off to dream
Or, luxury of moment's converse—
Of dreams most recently arisen, eyes
Beholding her in glorious morning light

COREY LEIGH

Matchless Beauty

Matchless beauty
Upon me lighting down
So firmly pressed, it's as if
I become dressed (nearly),
In gorgeous garments of her nudity
Ensuing, a sensual celebration
Effectually producing
Points of exclamation, which
Echo hallowed walls, love's room
Loud as voices of lightning
Bellowing thunderous tunes across stages of
Charcoal-gray-colored skies
Outside it's pouring
Almost as earsplitting as the roaring
Of fulfillment, taking place
Each instance our bodies integrate
Verbal proclamations of how much we care,
One for the other, fittingly resonate
Only, we don't stop there—
Having said what we mean, and
Meaning all we allege
Aptly, proof lies in passion
We proceed to demonstrate
Fury of such fashion
Leaves lungs for air greatly gasping
And limbs for more, innately grasping

Velvet Crush

Smooth as velvet (and so, so fine)
Soft as shiny moons in summertime,
Those silver-dollar-sized, and brightly,
Penetrating Georgia pines
Nightly, captive her body holds me
Eyes paralyzed in its design
Marinated in molasses,
Her feminine divinity caroling sweetly
Key of sex,
Train of thought off its track
Mental wreck, she keeps me
Lured, hooked in infatuation
Lost in lines of those curves
Sinker, her seductive flirtation
Reels in what little capacity curbed, any
Impulse to disregard margin
Upon seats of whim take wing
Enthralled amid such sensual arson
Dissolved in flares, her blistering sting—
Soprano of our climax, (in conclusion), chillingly sings

An Eye Unjaded

Tilted axis of my world
Everything now seen, more serene, different angles
Filled with passion over a girl
Relishing how she tediously untangled
A mangled, skeptic heart, knotted in disbelief
Traced in shame, shimmer-less shades of love
Jagged shards were all sizes and all shapes
White boards of heartache she aptly erased
Unmarked slate, how to love again, her tutelage demonstrates

Colored Purposeful

The other day
A friend calmly asked—
"What is it about her,
causing you to surrender your heart?"
I replied,
Unsure he'd even comprehend,
I gave nothing—
> It was always hers to have

He begged on—
"Exactly how'd you arrive,
destination of such realization?"
Again, I replied—
See . . . I was born, wept, and breathed
Of the womb torn, slept, and dreamed
During which time, God whispered—
> She, too, has been delivered

Perfect complement to my life—
Daughter of El Shaddai,
Faithfully trusted friend,
Fiercely loyal and committed partner
Eventual ever-loving wife, and
Mother of favored generations,
Grow in Him and her purity I'd come to know—
Therefore, deep meaning we display
Merely cause and effect preordained
Vibrancy of our bond, (onset to last breath)
> Of Elohim's brush, colored purposeful

COREY LEIGH

A Love Reclined

Sightlessly orbiting outer space
Eyeless inquires, satellites are seeing
How deeply I've sank
Emotional furnishings
Cozy fixture of life
Meeting you has meant—

Like a Fathers favorite chair,
Positioned in full recline,
Cushioned from a crazy world
At ease in your embrace
Relaxed if in your company
Unsettled any time absent

Comforted knowing
You support me in every way
Thoughts of returning home
To you hurriedly,
Highlight these stress-filled days—

    And nonsensical nights alike

Well Preserved

Romance lives—
From the grave, arisen
Were every mountain top tumbled
God's green earth disassembled
This very instant
Still
Residuals of idealism
Formless soul of love
Would surely see
All that's best of romanticism
Well preserved
Enshrined in bundles of amorous energy
Unfolding in phases
Reasserting itself
Even as centuries flow into ages
Continually—
From the grave, arisen
Romance lives on—
Perpetually reaffirmed

A Wanting You Invite

Charred clouds of my life
You pierced repeatedly
Because of you, pivotally hemorrhaging
Veins of new light—
Worlds seen more keenly
Enclosed in your insight
Emotionally empty to bursting sentimentally—
Surplus you incite

To be a better man
A wanting you invite—
Torch of time forged us friends
Bystanders covet our inseparable delight—
You cheerlead my dreams
As though they were your own
Not to mention, unconditional tailoring
Times it seems, at the seams, my life is unsown

Purity of your heart
Swells sails of our partnership
Together, entails ways we embark,
Maneuvering hindrances of monogamous commitment—
Were your essence ever scribed
Joy you bring, converted text
Scriptures, your influence would double as
Divine illustrations, by which all should abide

Watercolors

She colors me categorically
Euphoric hues of life, adoringly
Pouring out unto me, lovely the
Vibrant pail, her spiritual self
(From which she pours, of course)
Priceless, so pure of heart is she
As though coated in wealth
Canvas of me, enriched
Vein of her commitment
Drips, drizzled upon my person
Her artistry loaned itself uncommonly
Refurbishing, a heart hideously marred
In face of ache, those scars
Plastered in permanence
Proved too big a job
Toil, all others resolved far too challenging—
Ah, but look at me now . . .
In bows, her reign ascends my brow—
Sat upon relationship's easel
In garments of patience, she painted
Taking as much time as needed, to
Blend, mend, infuse, improve—
Seer of what was salvageable
Knower of what ought to be anew
And now, amid life's gallery
Onlookers admire, emphatically
Watercolors of our wedlock—
A matrimonial masterpiece

COREY LEIGH

A Love, Undyingly

Friends don't comprehend—
Since you came, they label me estranged
Mostly, I just grin
Were it I outside peering in—
It's plausible, I'd peg me the same

Beneath thinly threaded brows
Relax loveliest fluorescent browns
Ever to lay upon faces of mankind
Through which, encouragement so shines
Even the most improbable, illogical
Aspirations endure, even now optional
Blades of ambition and dream
Forever gorgeous green
Decorated in warmth—
Sun of your always reassuring gaze

Ink of your spirit
Effervescent hue of optimism
Your positivity exudes
Even as heavy air of struggle
Balloons, burdens giving reason
To call it quits, leaving, scales of life teetering
Despite misfortunes' bulk
You never seem to sulk
With whatever may come, you cope—
More than rubbed off on me

I wear symbolisms of hope as sleeves
Tattooed in the upbeat outlook of
Your inner self's artistry

Comfort casting
Buttons of invincibility unfastening
Permissible to appear emotionally unclothed
Soil of your acceptance sustains growth
Toil of your affection contains both
Oversized ego and restless heart of mine
Replanted, watered, and pruned
Natural light, plane of your soul astral
Upon its wings, temple of my being tilted
Leaning lovingly toward solar sourced energy—
Otherwise known as your love for me, undyingly

Cater to You

Smile baby, smile
As each minute descends
Drawing to a close
À la curtains on a stage
Your busy work week
Which, and I quote
Worked your last nerve—

Off the clock, officially
Relax your mind
As you head home
In a tub of thoughts more peacefully
Similar to the one your body's
Soon to be slipped into
Bath water pouring
Lavender bubbles nearby
Scented candles rehearsing their lullaby
Stella Rosa, chilled the way you like
Italian dishes simmer upon the stove
Sade, as only she can
Soothes the mood in song
Like trains of evening dresses,
Her lyrics flow out in stereo
Massage oils await
Tell me where it hurts, and
These hands will kiss and make it better
My perfect present

Paper wrapped in your silk robe
Posturepedic sleigh bed, your dessert
Sink your teeth in and sleep
This weekend you deserve to rest
Evident in your eyes
Hard work over looked by many
Hasn't gone unnoticed in mine
In accordance, allow me then, to cater to you—
Privileged I even can
Proud of all you goal and achieve
Prouder still to be considered your man

So, smile baby, smile—
As each minute descends
Drawing to a close
À la curtains on a stage
Your busy work week
Which, and I quote
Worked your last nerve

Sweet Lady

Sweet Lady—
Disrobe your inhibitions
Bare to me your soul
Latch on to intuition
As lengths of our love unfolds
Gowned in nudity, fittingly adorned—
Your own moisturized mahogany
Radiant, beautifully worn
Given ample opportunity
Predisposed explorer in me
Overdosed in discovery
Craving hands raise anchor and set sail
Propelled curvature of your frame
Deliberate journey, crown to soles
Every erogenous zone in between—
A wondrous scene to be seen
As not all fruit falls from trees
In the flesh, peeled rinds of attire
Mouth of me waters witnessing
Ripeness of desire, freshly squeezed
Wetter than christenings, you bless me
Overlapping limbs, you stretch me
Out, across mattresses of innermost fantasies
A back so arched, it's as if earth itself reclined
For some reason, I do dream in rhyme
Your soul leafless, ushers me in

.

TRIBUTE TO A WOMAN

Seating every line, yes
Beauty is thy name
Your guard shelved, threadbare
Celestial figure, blank as an unmarked page—
Allow quills of my lips please
To ink upon you poetry—
Countless kisses cursively written—
Bodily inscriptions erotically engraved

Vintage

On shelves of satisfaction
Sit bottled up fantasies (say love . . .)
Why age what you crave most?
Cast-iron keys of a tryst
Unlocks her caged soul
We uncork and pour toasts
Under pressure of pleasure
Vintage, wines of her aspirations
Sparklingly implode
Caught between partial preference,
Sit back and sip or greedily gulp . . .
(Both of a mind to)
Flavor of savor
Sees our hopes
(Pinned tail of its coat)
Carried away, inebriated lush
Aching back of fantasy
Deeply massaged, fulfillments touch
Tender, accessory to enticement
I surrender, folds that blind
Cords that bind, stricken lash
Erotic role players
Our senses splash, crossing paths
Spilled in thrills of indulgence
Carnally fostered
Slow roasted, a pinnacle approaches
Incubated spiritedly, in fervor of the moment

TRIBUTE TO A WOMAN

In Evening (When Suns Go Down)

She lessens all the lights—
Instantaneously,
Watery rains of darkness
Upon our room descend
Drenching thoroughly all within,
Leaving walls plastered in pastel
Blackened even—
Steadiest of hands
Suitable of any operating room
Tending to her Meng robe and wares
Surgically, each piece removed
In glory of the nude
We both stand, parallel—
Air of lusty eyes
Nearly burst desire, it balloons
Off a cliff, her flavorsome kiss
Heart rate rapid, my pulse parasailed—
Sightless, hands peruse her body as braille
Reading between lines, her curves do tell
In whispers of quivers
Her geese laying skin, she shivers—
Harmonious aloud, moans do sing
Jingle bells of our bedroom alarmingly ring
Red nose of pleasure led
Tempo slow, snow-driven sleigh bed
So deep beneath Egyptian sheets, we become the threads

COREY LEIGH

Given, one to another
Total, sums of ourselves—
Gift wrapped in satisfaction
Garments of her generousness
Clothe my indulgence
Her appetite for sensual
A belly well fed—
As fowlers, casting finale's net
Cuddled up closely, we commence
To track down, catch our very own breaths

Velvet Sky

Against backdrops of velvet sky
Diamond-like, stars assuredly shine
Every curve, your silhouette supreme
Silvery, entirely outlined

Your hair, you let down, naturally
Curls unfurl, bearing likeness of weeping trees
Dizzied in appeal of your faculty
Scent of your hair a song, along I hum gleefully

Cool moisture of your kiss
A softly drizzled mist, preludes of erotic rain
Falls and settles upon leaves of my lips
Stemmed in excitement, pleasure sustains

Laid beneath your maneuvering
Lines between actuality and vision blur
Lacking remark, yet intuitively soothing
Well into the night, our bodies converse

Colored in joyful moans, expertise of your artistry
Portrait of culmination rousingly revealed
Chills of release blanket blistering flames, charring me
Indescribable best defines, one for the other, feelings we feel

COREY LEIGH

M-A-N in Her Middle

From foundation of the world
Throughout and beyond all eternity—
An urgent emergency, I desire to become,
That which I assuredly was always foretold to be—
The *M-A-N,* (her one and solely)
Positioned prominently, and held responsibly
Smack-dab in the center of (and reinforcing)—
Her *R-O-C-E*

Greatest Gift

No tissue paper lining
Insides of shiny bags

No bows, nor laced ribbons
Receipt-less, unpriced tags

No boxes draped in velvet
Neither Tiffany's hue

No *close your eyes* necessary
Special delivery couldn't do

Justice, a man's most valuable possession
Totality of himself— completely, freely, true

None deemed worthy but one—
To which all of me awarded, exclusively unto you

Charms

Figaro necklaces of commitment
From which our hearts do hang
Separate links, neither weak
Molten friendship—
Golden relationship—
Unified and refined
Forged of one accord
Chaining singularity,
Clasping our ties romantically, and
Charmingly accentuating our bond—
In tandem, quite dandily

Relation's Ship

I could feel my heart sink
 Endlessly lessening
 Such a useless anchor
  Stubborn pride became—

Reborn whenever present
 In presence of her beauty,
 Depth of her person
  Deeper than oceanic flooring

Very breath of me, leapt
 Willfully, overboard
 Walking planks of emotion
  Falling into feelings never known—

Weightless, vulnerability rafts makeshift
 Watercourses of heartache prior
 More keenly navigated, forward, her
  Altruistic soul encompassing northward

COREY LEIGH

Philosophically

Where else would I be, if not
Held long within your gaze?
I am merely the heart of an astronomer
Lost and found among the stars—

    Aside from the sun
        None brighter than the two
            Perfectly set upon your face

Of what else would I think, if not
Rhetorically enticed in part?
I am merely the mind of a philosopher
Q & A-ing ideals you embody—

    As qualities' possibilities are pondered
        Thoughts of what a woman should be
            Answers reach ends where you start

How else would I be seen, if not
Through concentrated focus of your lens?
I am merely the film of a photographer
Rosily immortalizing a moment—

    Thornless you thrive
        Protruding concrete heart of mine
            Of acts unnatural, authentic love stems

Lake Minnetonka

Lovers
I have seen
Plunge
Headfirst
Fully immersed in majesty
Reveling amid rippling
Once mild-mannered waters

Others
I have seen
Marvel
Momentarily
Tenderly touching their toes
Commitment's computation, analyzing afore
Exactly what must be endured

Variations exist, yet
Entrance among these waters
Remains doubtlessly inevitable
Therefore, it's imperative to forewarn—

Careless and cautious alike
In an instant, each end up overtaken—

Completely consumed, process of love's purification

COREY LEIGH

Illumined Femininity

Initial outset,
First minute of first moment
Fatedly we met
Discerning eyes, astutely aware
In you resonating
Such a glorious and gorgeous light,
Evidence of the very same
Many moons before when,
Author of all nature commanded, let there be—
Earliest day, actively on our behalf
He saw it fit to exercise His creativity
Authoritatively decreed and severed in half
Day from night
And now, all that's best of dark and light
Reside magnificently in spiritual synergy of illumed femininity
Your godly-gated community
To which you've blessed me access, privy to—
I vow to make fruitful use of said privileges, no misuse

Hunger Games

Choice weaponry
Bow and arrow of her sex appeal
Supreme mastery, she wields tirelessly
Waging war against my senses
Often, seizing control encountering
Slightest bit of resistance, employing
Chemical warfare, weaponized
Her slender body baptized
Lagoons of favored fragrances
She doesn't play fair, of rooms
Entering and exiting at her whim
And yet, in arrears, her scent loiters here
With me, defenses descend swiftly—

Subconsciously
My inner self swoons as she croons
To any tune top of mind
Sentimental songbird, her Neo-soul uncaged
Unharnessing harmonies
Alarmingly, Cupid's gate teasingly unhinged
Jovial vocals, pathos provoking,
Covertly encompassing sensation
Masquerading as well-intentioned melody,
Half the battle already hers—

Strategic, slipping on and off, various Vicki Secrets
According to her, all in an effort to

Determine perfect permutation, only
As lustful eyes look on, scenic
This route in which she carries on, deviant
Glossed over, wishful gaze
Sore eyes tortured, she layers in lace—

Candy-coated curves, effervescently starburst
Then, dressed in black, Miss Mary Mack, attired in sunshade
Thermostat of my being, blood boils,
Manly region rallied
Her palm presses upon my front, blacksmithing
Fashioning a flinch, she seductively asking
If I would be so kind as to zip her up—

Enough!
Will weakened, I manage to muster up, and
Courageously confront, one grand stand,
Crayon akin to, lips coloring nape of her neck
Contractual moan, she begins to submit to—
All at once, summoning strength to regroup, she
Seals promises of postpone, sensuous kiss
Taste alone lends itself semi-victorious—

Scarred, but alive to tell the story
Hungrily warring in this fashion every single morning

TRIBUTE TO A WOMAN

125

Preying

First time we met
You became the object of my desire—
I knew right away, I wanted to be yours

An unidentifiable something
Seemed to latch hold
And at present, defiantly refuses to let go

Admittedly, I don't want it to—
Unsure of how you managed to execute
Yet, content to concede

I can't get over you—
Forever entangled in this web you've spun,
Mannishly anticipating each instance, you make me yours

Stormy Rhetoric

Temptation speaks—
Strident, universal tongue
Its gripping narrative
Offers psyches inebriated in allure
Occasion to succumb,
Sober minds oft disapprove
Of veiled caution, be thou removed
Unfasten restraint, aimed to obscure
Give in to me, every respect
Release captive of your impulse
Trust stimulation's inclination
Desire's pulse felt quickening, metaphorically caressed
A face flushed, inward lanterns of lust rekindling
Beneath chimneys of self-fulfillment
Terrific fires are just the beginning—
Refuse not, opportune invitations to attend
Sensation's engagement,
To proposed unlimited merriment, merely tap in
Discontinue tightrope walks to finish lines of satisfied,
Teetering upon the cusp of every mounting urge,
Eager for your arrival, so anxiously
True ecstasy looms, awaiting impatiently
In waters emphatically outspoken, ragingly stirred
Submerge your inhibitions, by all means
Allow yourself permission, to be swept away—
Born of elation, tidal waves of displacement
Wholly overtaken, stormy rhetoric of temptation

Pyramids of Her Apparel

Building blocks of her apparel
Wardrobe deliberately contrived
Savage Fenty's finest lace, its
Handcrafted page
Precedes rough draft of dress-up
Composition of her curves sexily outlined
Supporting foundation of her fullness
From there
She stabilizes base of her wares
Further, her syrupy-chocolate lower half
Fills brim of milk's glass
Seemingly, garnished in her silky-white slip
Just as quick, she dips
Fountain pen of her body sips and absorbs
Ink of her ash-colored skirt
And brick-red blouse
Ringside I sit
Awaiting main event
Moment she attempts
To pull her V-neck sweater
Over her head, without toppling her curls
High rise of her garments
Shake in winds of awkwardness
But as always, she does it
Short, lives the accomplishment
As herd of her attention

COREY LEIGH

128

Becomes rounded up
In application of accessories
She layers neck and wrists
Crowning point of outfit's pyramid—
In company of her construction
I revert to mannerisms of a child
Wherein, what goes up, must come down
Joy derived in erecting edifices
Excitement of such assembly unrivaled,
Were it not for thrills of witnessing demolition—
Under influence of desire, her attire I'm dismantling,
A layer at a time,
Her clothes come tumbling down
Frantically, scattering grounds of our bedroom
A well-fashioned wonder, covetously reduced to rubble—
A rescue unwarranted, considering extent of her enjoyment

Late Nights, Early Mornings

More Princely than *Purple Rain*
Chorus lines downpouring
Electric love stories
Masterfully unfolding
Upon my lips her kisses dwell
Flowers of excitement
Flourishingly swell
Surface protruding
Stemmed in lust, alluding
Gardens of gratification
Ballooning
Human nature's helium
Manly stars arise, warm
As interior of her paradise
Centerpiece of pleasure
Smooth, as rods of lightning
Pierced skies of her thighs
Melodic, downpours of her body
Each note vocalized
In scales of her sighs
Take a bow beautiful
Echoes of elation
Encamped currently
On cusp of an encore, en route
Hurrying over horizons of another round

Lost in Love

Ways in which she loves
So lost I've become
Sparkling stones and breadcrumbs
Neither trail capable of
Recovering the person, I was once
Prior to, stumbling upon
Breadth of her love, limitless—
Unsullied within it, washed anew
Laundered serenity of her semblance
Lost in, and getting back to
Revelations of love, newfound glimpses

TMC (The Marathon Continues)

Seeker of companionship
Amid annual marathons
Aptly disguised as life—
My soul, runner of its course
Found you to be its finish line,
Crossing your path—
Completion my grandest prize

Hindsight

Arms ache in wake of your absence
Unable to behold that which they covet most
Empty, as starless skies, yet wishing you were near
A pang so prolonged, the body is of a mind to
Sever ties completely, divorcing its self of the two,
Invariably
Sensing such a sadistic sentiment
Inwardly aloud
The soul assumes role of reason, and
Its voice-over carries weight (cause and effect of which)
Off planks of realization
Walks a thought . . .
Cemented in clarity, at long last allowing
Perspective to sink in—
Within the heart itself
Innumerable memories are nestled, as newborns
So lovingly held they are—
Wrapped in silken swaddles of affection
A godly green, glows leaves of your laughter
Protruding branches of private thoughts,
My heart's garden their eternal dwelling place—
Within the heart itself
Upon every beating page, joy you left behind
Nostalgically pens your name, permeating
Additional documentation, proof of a time you were mine
Within the heart itself

TRIBUTE TO A WOMAN

And on the verge of bursting
Storehouses remain, stocked overly
A testament, of all which was gleaned
Garden of Eden of your being
Fields of your will, vineyards of your esteem—
Within the heart itself
Resides in and of itself, lessons of love
Of which, clearly you were led into my life to teach,
I have both learned and discerned—

Although belatedly

Answered Prayer

In her is like—
Romance reaffirmed
Air of commitment, cleanly crisp
All of me given, a favor returned
Routinely, comfort of her love I exist
Daily, she has a way of
Making me feel
Alive, as though always for the very first time
Her vibrant smile
Electrocutes dreaming eyes of mine
Her touch adoring
Soft as summer breezing through chimes
Sends me soaring
My senses sing in rhyme
Upon rungs of her devotion, I cling
Both ambition and dream do climb
Her support much like a ladder
Enthused, myself I lose
Four corners of her encouragement
Dexterity, only in the Maker's realm
Pottery of His artistry
Creation of one such as she
Paired lovingly, affirmation of prayers years prior
Outpoured longingly
In her arms now reaffirmed—
Belongingly

TRIBUTE TO A WOMAN

135

Fluorescent

Her smile beams bright—
Resplendently soft
Silvery light
Of semi-sized moons
Subtle, symbolizes manner
Which she consumes
Pervading elements of dark
Chasing away shadows
My somber mood
Set upon its heels
As tearful turned to cheerful—
She saw sadness subdued

Unshackled, free of fearful's cocoon
Fearless wings see to bring
A heart once reeling
Weighted down in reservation,
Sense of liveliness renewed
Hastening, absent any hint of hesitation—
Unafraid to soar, heightening evermore
Aim of endless love,
Myself forever climbing
Passageways—

Her smile fluorescently lighting

Temptation's Symphony

In the hush of noon, you are stationary waters
Neighboring pastures of me, glowing green
Heart beneath your breast
Snare drum, it thumps
Rhythmically
You remain at rest, weightlessly
Your cheek, my chiseled chest, to the other,
Cozily pressed, pasted peacefully—
As you lay, in figures of eight
Gold seal revolution blades, my fingertips skate
Copiously coloring space
Between small of your back and shoulder blades
Your head laid, lightly
Slightly under my chin
Warm, exhales nibble away at my neck
Sense of smell breached, subsequently overtaken
Scent of your hair seeping in—
Grasp of self-control, loosening
Breath of restraint harder to hold
Sinking in pools of persistent movement, ripple effects
Begotten as you, not quite yet awakened, adjust
Lower extremities, smoothly brushing against mine own
Of a sudden, temptation's symphony
Upon stage of my fixation, plays pleasingly
Entangled in arousal's ability to persuade
For indulgence sake
I, beg pardon of your dreams
From which, I must now ravenously tear you away

TRIBUTE TO A WOMAN

Pillow Talk

Incense lit
One for each corner of the room
Born of ash, powdery pirouettes, each begets
Fine particles encircling the mood
Forbidden fruit flavorsome
Georgia's prettiest peach,
Ripeness peaked, plum sweet
Honey child, her
Sunkissed skin so goldenly brown
Cast in cocoons of sheer lingerie,
Sparkly red fishnet bodysuit, see it removed
Bedroom butterfly
Come closer now as we partake, apiece
Pleasurable, the give and take
Of lust, two selves cemented
Merely pined for at first, now concrete
Grant me permission please
To climb and kiss you there
Crystal stairs of those thighs
Thereby, I, an engineer
Accountably held for the arch
Suspending your body finely in air
Equipped with all the right weaponry
Handsomely she handles me
Doves ceremoniously flown, trumpets blown, honoring
Try to resist, ultimately submit

Allegiance, her sensual sovereignty
To which I pledge
Neck-deep in seas of pride
Overtaken in her tide
Yet, still I beg
Bedroom masochist
Treading waters, my fellow Aquarian
Her cups runneth over
Pitchers of pleasure poured overly
Walls closing in
Her grip tightens, explosively
Yield to her will, captivated soberly
Joyful moans a fountain pen
Addendums of indulgence aptly authorized—
Her sex appeal so signature, pleasingly
We inscribe sighs on dotted lines of an aromatic evening

TRIBUTE TO A WOMAN

Cater to You (My Second Reply)

From a hard day's work
Home, love let me welcome you
Rare to hear it there, I know
So, this is me thanking you—
From time you arose
It's been nonstop multitasking
Such tedious balancing involved
Hardly afforded a sec to
Hear yourself think
Much less, collect your own thoughts—
Stressed out and so tired
Allow me to alleviate
Heaviness, demands your day
Heaved upon you,
As exasperation dissolves
My resolve, simply reminding you
You are so loved and admired—
Ever you're here with me
My company doubles as
A golden guarantee
Meaning, no matter what
You will always be, categorically
Adored upon arrival—
Days like this, I wait patient for
Opportunity to foster
An appreciative environment

COREY LEIGH

For starters
I say we have a seat, and
From equation of aggravation
Perhaps subtract those heels, and
Lay in my lap your feet—
Or how about
Letting your hair down love, and
Setting your head upon my shoulder
Actively I'll listen, while
You unmask irritating elements
Which, sought to conceal *full*
From *beauty* of your day

Playing Fields of Monogamy

Playing fields of monogamy, underprivileged
Many a relationship ran its course and failed
Sharpened cleats of our commitment, not to mention—
Cushy insoles of compromise, sees us prevail

Pushing always, one another to be our best selves
Upon a portion of life's scale
Each other's biggest constructive critic—
Opposite end measured alike
Each other's biggest support system
Evenly balanced, in it together, equal parts, debit and credit

Persistently challenged, an oft wavering society
Knowingly or otherwise, promotes mass mishandling—
Divisive individualism, absentee spiritualism, not to mention,
Standing ovations for displays of promiscuity—
Damaging, each corrodes exclusivity of matrimony

Institute of family, morally, its fabric bearing stains,
Uneasy to remove, fortunately, reemphasizing values
Offers opportunity to redress, a steadier structure reframed,
Leveled fields, once stunted culturally, growth spurts resume
I'm grateful, together, recommitted to overcome, taller we stand

On Your Birthday
(Inspired by M. Gordon)

Just wanted to take a second
To wish you
A very happy birthday—
In spirit
With you, I celebrate—
Were it not for your beginning,
My heart presently I fear
Would not recognize its own reflection
Absent mirror of your love—
I hope your day is
Every bit as lovely and special
As I perceive you yourself to be—
If not more even,
As that depth of perception
Assuredly defies gravity of description

Morning Birds

Center stage, early autumn trees—
Cued amid colors, such orange rust, greenly golden leaves
Morning birds, my heart mirroring, sweetly sing
Concertedly, songs amplify distinctly
All I find myself for you presently feeling—
Immersed in sentimental seasons newly begun
My *Bravebird*, as Amel Larrieux once foretold in *For Real*
I too, can tell of our fortunes—
A wealth of romantic times to come

COREY LEIGH

Confirmation

To the one's I've loved—
Absent avail
Ones of whom weary befell,
Overwrought and couldn't quite tell
If what they thought I felt
Was ever really real . . .

Result of (and for sake of avoiding ache)
My heart overcautiously clothed, pride-laced veil
Never once lifted, solemnly until
I finally learned to accept, trust and express
Feelings fear formally divested, yet
Deep down I always cared, incalculably, yes

Parasols

Although mistrustful eyes
Are prone to look on
Long, rather intently
Yours, I intend
To keep unacquainted with weary—
Worry none my love
Rest those watchful eyes
I'll keep you safely shaded
As temperatures of doubt
Reverse their rise—
Seasons of liars prior have passed
Sown seed of commitment
In me, a tree fully bloomed
One near water, rooted
Simultaneous possession
Its energy, both potential and kinetic
Both budding and fruit-bearing branches
Comfort casting, evergreen
Tarp to a troublesome sun
Shone of foolish men
Rejoice, advantage takers are of your past
Halt, this instant, learned defense mechanism
Resulting, such a persistent strain
Useless, as you consider our future—
My timeline proven
Track record tested

COREY LEIGH

Never said and not meant
And anything asked
Of myself first demanded—
So now, sleep soothingly my love
Rest those watchful eyes
Allow yourself to dream
In peace, permissibly—
Marked safe, from past toxic masculinity
Parasol of my commitment
Shielding idyllically

Hands of Time

Hands of time
Should be placed in casts—
Kisses of yours, anytime
Anywhere, deserve to last

Sugary sweet
Soft as winter snow first falling
As if kisses could speak—
Love's name continuously calling

My soul is a flowerbed
Your lips are April's rain
Wardrobe of wilting I've shed
Reinvigorated, burgeoning all over again

Stripped down, completely bare
Whirlpools of a kiss, hearts bathe
Heavily soaked, watermarking air
Lovingly afloat, laws of gravity gravely betrayed

I Dream Different

I dream different—
In a sense, souls in love don't sleep
Dawn of anticipation, ever imminent
I see shelves of tomorrow
Fully stocked, possibilities unlimited
As far as our bond is concerned

Roots of our relationship
Grow deep as maple trees
Ingredients such as
Communication, trust, willingness to compromise
Keeps ship of our relation syrupy sweet

Minus blue prints and hardhats
You turned out to be an architect
Hands in every draft of the man
I was designed and destined to become

In my life, joy you spread
Wide as eagle's wings
In flight, we glide
Above all petty impediments
My very own, you are the archetype
Of every sentimental sentiment

There isn't a passport known to man
Offering clearance
Necessary for visits, so far out of limits
Heights our love is headed
See, you are the difference
Allowing me to dream different—

Because souls in love don't sleep

Lanterns of Hope

You are the spark
Which lit within me
Lanterns of hope
Whose usages were rendered
Useless, for quite some time—
Your requisite arrival
Allowed dense fog of lonesomeness
To gradually recede—
In so doing
Curtains of disbelief arose
Prominently cued in your spotlight
Center stage, faith stood
Meritorious monologue, captivating
Inescapably resonating auditorium of my being
Floor to mezzanine of my spirit—
Roaring vociferously—
Bravo! Bravo! Bravo!
Accordingly
You have afforded me
Opportunity to remove
Mask of invincibility
For so long, worn all too well
All facades aside, you offer freedom
Internal weaknesses no longer unaddressed
Maturity unchained, barricades of emotional unavailability
No longer an encumbrance

My very own outlet
You've reacquainted me with previously disregarded
Certitudes and sentiments, a new outlook on
What a loving, healthy, committed relationship can be—
Creative expression's advocate
Your love, a rich and fiery color pallet
Brush-stroking canvas of my life
You are the reality
For which dreams even exist
Spilled ink of ever-loving affection
Page of my heart
Your fingerprint bearing—
An unremitting kindling
Innermost lanterns of love brilliantly ablaze
Hope-filled still, effect of your spark
Flames of restored faith forever inflates

 **Oftentimes**

Oftentimes when we're together
I'm afraid to be myself—
I fear the real me, may not yet be
Worthy and deserving, of a woman
As wonderfully dynamic as yourself

(You see) I like you—
In the highest, most-purest form,
Possibilities of you, constantly considering
I smile wide as every ancestor
Imagining life more abundantly of those thereafter
Pondering unwearyingly
One of these days—
Your heart will be mine

You, you are sensitive, yet strong
Gentle and genuine as well—
Regal divinity of your person, radiantly arrayed,
Inside and out—
Reciprocal beauty,
Altar of romanticism, sacrificial, declarations displayed
Earnestly, I pray you never ever change

Subtle ways you look at me
An ever-listening ear lent willfully,
Of wisdom and positivity, your speech heavily steeped
Childlike laughter and honeycombed kisses,
Innately, remnants of each lasts inwardly

TRIBUTE TO A WOMAN

Woman, I care for you deeply—
Seeded preciously within me sprout feelings
Mustard seeds to Sequoia Hyperion trees
Maturing all the more, emergent in
Dew-filled dawns of each new day

Yolanda's Second Psalm
(Inspired by & dedicated to Y. Parker)

In one breath, you were equally
The greatest gain—
Greatest loss of my life
Never did I dream
Heaven's favor—
Such a blessing
Would be bestowed upon me—
If only for an instant
Actually,
Quiet as it's kept
Those were my dreams
Unexpected expectations if you will
(And, so to speak)
A wish so wanted
Vivid eyes of imagination
Could barely see
As quickly as you came
The phrase, *gone too soon*
Rates cheap in comparison
To priceless wonders
You exuded
While you were here, (particularly with me)—
You once asked, I be your friend first
Willingly I agreed
All the while, masquerading uncertainty

Unsure exactly, how that was to be done
Given immense magnitude, of
My sorely more wanting heart—
Inwardly, I smiled
Almost as brilliantly
As you yourself, were known to
Monumental moment I realized
All I had to do was be unto you
That which in turn, you were first unto me—
A friend, in the purest sense
Very definition indeed—
In one breath you were
The greatest gain—
Greatest loss of my life
And though your absence
At times paralyzing
I take comfort in knowing
I get to find in you again someday
My greatest gain . . .
A foundation of friendship
Whose construction was so cruelly interrupted
Demolishing high rise of our relationship—
Leaving, so many things shared between us
Lost among debris of your untimely passing

COREY LEIGH

In All Honesty

True love—
Won't ever forsake you
Stirs and never shakes you
Bends but never breaks you
Tremors yet never quakes you
Won't over coals,
Ever attempt to rake you
Will in no way
Impulsively seek to replace you
Will comfort and embrace you
Won't misuse nor of advantage, take you
Derives pleasure in who you are
Never tries to reshape you
Wholeheartedly lends its support
Of your dreams, and won't ever awake you
Encourages your every endeavor
Comprehends your worth, as such, appreciates you
Challenges and motivates you
Deemed fraudulent if ever it degrades you
Fallacious still
If of your mistakes, never fully forgave you
Should uplift and never shame you
Rushes to compromise, unhurried to blame you
Allows you to build upon friendship
Its foundation remains stable
Is less about criticism, more inclined to praise you

Won't for granted take you
Serves as adhesive, ever
Hardships seek to separate you
Unable to demean, rather
Relishes the need to celebrate you
Forever an antonym of ungrateful
Won't rest on laurels of loyal
Labors habitually to remain faithful—
Discovery of this and more in you
Finds me forever thankful, in all honesty
Gospel of your love so true
Religiously I praise you!

COREY LEIGH

Trade in My Life

By your side
Laying
While you sleep, I look on
Praying—
If in the morning light
Window of our world, all is no longer right
And darkness devours bright
Or, if of lids which won't ajar
And, of our dreams we lose sight
Temporal vessels, of ourselves no longer withheld
Earthly to astral, our souls disrobe
Ascending new dimensions, in flight
Astronomical planes, a paradoxical paradise
Invitation only, biblical book of life
Guest list amassed meritoriously
If for some reason, our names unwritten
Disallowed of Heaven's gates, I'd pry with all my might
Unrelenting, absolutely no surrendering without a fight
Unholy war I'd wage, on your behalf
Absent reservation, joyously trade in my life
Resiliently, risk it all
If in the end you alone gained entrance
Outcome of otherworldly efforts,
I'd be more than satisfied
Subsequent consequence fully accepted
Contented, voluntarily suffering an eternity
So long as you didn't

TRIBUTE TO A WOMAN

Untitled

Let not your heart be troubled—
no score keeper needed
die won't be cast either, as
this *level of commitment* is no game

Allow your trust to wade within me—
while probing waters of man's deeds
words weighted often sink, and so
amidst actions, truth is preserved

Under the influence of love—
some things said and done
sober hearts would surely shun, therefore
grounds of forgiveness are forever brewing

Relationships remain a marathon—
those most swift aren't assured crowns
stamina of friendship allows us to endure
obstacles, many others prove unable to sustain

All the days of my life—
expect to be celebrated in its entirety
you were, are, and always will be, *the exception*
a rarity, only *you* know what I mean

COREY LEIGH

Resurrection Blue

(And on the third day)
All I could do was
Throw my hands toward Heaven's way
Mercy me, my love
Thinks it best we go our separate ways—
Anything but that Lord
Let not our book close, rather, pen a new page
Down on my knees
Gorgeously please, somehow, someway—
My baby back home Lord
      Hoist what we had beyond the grave

I can do better
In fact, before You, I vow it this day
Should have never taken her for granted
Your daughter deserved better—
Exclusivity of my attention, not to mention
Fairer measures of my time
Although belatedly
I've come to comprehend
The in-betweens of life and loss
True love is not a given, and
Ever established, ought to be
Gazed upon as privilege
      Conclusively, my God, I get it!

Therefore, humbly I implore thee
Aid and abet me, please
Three hundred and fifty-nine degrees
Circumference of my mistakes
Don't let me
Secure another cycle of transgression
Rather, see said circle broken—
Roll away stone, signify resurrection
Bid us bloom, all the more beautiful
In your ways, replanted—
I'm down on my knees
Gorgeously please, somehow, someway
My baby back home Lord—
      Hoist what we had beyond this grave

Sentiments of a Man

As time continues to pass—
Tallied in dozens, abandoned by waysides
Tattered pages, torn asunder
Consecutive calendar years
Unceremoniously eulogized
I find it increasingly difficult
To express fully
That which has built up inside of me
An entire eternity it seems—
Perhaps the fact that
There is so much I wish to relay
Makes it nearly impossible
To all at once
Disperse this mass of information
On accounts of, amassed communications
Previously known to myself solely—
Perhaps the fact that
You are someone I call friend
Makes it harder all the more
For me to say things freely as I feel
In fear of jeopardizing
This bond we certainly share—
Perhaps the fact that
Manicured lawns of pastimes are littered
In inadequate attempts
Of unsuccessful efforts to convey similar sentiment

Only to be met with picketed resistance,
Developed into discouragement
Which I so desperately seek to shed—
Truly you are special
In my eye
As well as all the world's—
Qualities you possess
Are more often than naught
Highly sought, yet seldomly realized—
Occasionally you are dreamlike
Attainable in one grasp
Yet so far out of reach on the other
Full pursuit of such paradox
At times a bit surreal—
I guess reality of it all
Is that, with time and persistence
Wildest of dreams can come true
(Perhaps faith and patience are prerequisites as well)
Anyway, the point is—
For years you've been my dream
More so recently than ever before
Full disclosure— I love you (you know that)
Always have, always will— (you are aware as well)
As I grow older
So, too, intensity of these feelings—
As it presently stands
My love for you is immeasurable
Steadfast and immovable
It scares and thrills me all at once,

COREY LEIGH

More than I've ever cavalierly let on—
Harkened days of distant pasts
Outfitted in remembrance
Dapper memories, somewhat similar sentiments
Little known, yet you once revealed to me
Patterned feelings, fashioned of your own
Emotional sewing machine—
Arithmetic of your admission unfolding as follows . . .
Upon parabola of warmhearted regard,
You've plotted me lifelong friend
Abacus of your untarnished heart counts me loved, and
Theorems of attraction
Spiritual, physical, mental, and emotional,
Yours for me, plus mine conversely,
For years you wished were longingly squared away—
Yet, at a time when you felt as though
In my possession, your vulnerability would be least safe
Admittedly you sensed adequately
As I was proudly noncommittal
Pleasure derived remaining unavailable emotionally
Of your own accord, unraveling shrouds of secrecy
You, in your own time conveying, unbeknownst to me
Not only did you joyously foresee,
Your preference of life in love always included me—
I do not doubt for a second
At that time, that was what you meant
However, times, as well as people, change
Hopefully
You haven't moved on completely

TRIBUTE TO A WOMAN

Hopefully
You haven't changed to the point where
Eyes of our history never come to see
Bluer skies and newer moons of possibility
Hopefully,
Somewhere inside of you
An inkling of all the afore still resides
Perhaps resurfacing even as you read this—
(Or soon thereafter, whatever the case may be)
Ultimately, I'd like to develop
A more mature relationship
Another level,
One which we have yet to explore
A deeper, more meaningful bond,
Segueing into commitment—
As an aside, I used to wonder why
Or how, we seemed to get along so well
I always deemed it to be because
We were alike in so many ways . . .
Now I'm not so sure . . .
I think now, ways in which we differ
Provides privilege for us to coincide as well as we do—
People come and go everyday
Yet, after all this time you've remained true
Do you know how hard that is to find?
In a world where people grow apart
Faster than they come together
What we have is special, a rarity indeed
And though I'm grateful for our friendship
I think it would be a shame

COREY LEIGH

166

If we were never anything more—
Therefore, regarding regal grace of your esteem
Permit me please to lay forever at your feet
My imminent adoration and unrelenting love—
Honeycombed in humility, (and yours solely)
My heart wholly, goldenly on its knees

Acknowledgements

All praise to the Most High, my greatest source of inspiration, from whom all blessings flow, and with whom all things are possible. From initial vision to final manifestation, I concertedly channeled His spirit of creativity, and am exceedingly pleased with the outcome. To God be the glory, forever.

An infinite thanks once again to my late mother, Brenda Love. Her motherly love, endless sacrifice, inexhaustible support, and constant encouragement will last a lifetime. She alone knew how much this book meant to me, just as, though departed, I alone know how much the actuality of this moment means to her! I know in heavenly places, she's even prouder of her son!

To my angel, Yolanda Parker, when you passed, so too a part of me. However, your influence lives on mightily. I still vividly recall all we shared, our late nights on the phone while I read aloud various poems, and the pieces I penned specifically for and gifted unto you. Certainly, you share in this dream, and your name lives on in part. Knowing you are smiling down, this very moment, is joyous.

To everyone that purchases a copy of and reads this book of mine, there are no words to adequately exemplify the gratitude I feel. Your support means more than the world to me, more than you could ever comprehend! You are all such blessings; I consider you my destiny helpers! I pray blessings are measured back to you in greater multiples.

A very special, heartfelt thanks to Melissa Cheng, who graciously served as associate editor and advisor. Your input during final stages of publication was critical. Coincidentally, years prior, your belief in me as a writer led to my first job in New York. I am forever grateful.

A huge thanks to Meesha Howard, whose proofreading services, Eye-Proofread, was truly a God-send. I appreciate all the time, energy, and effort you expended, immensely.

With the utmost regard, I am extremely thankful for Ana Marinovic, for her incredibly amazing artwork and cover design. Ana, you easily exceeded expectations, bringing my vision to life, and delivering an iconic cover. I'm so glad to have collaborated with you.

To my photographer, Vlad Satori, thanks so much for capturing such a dope and aptly fitting portrait of me. You're equally an amazing photographer and person.

To all others I've lost along the way, in your memories as well, I am proud to have accomplished this goal. Most notably, my grandmother, the late Mrs. Rosie Mae, coach Mark Whittinghill, and my dear friend, Lauren Savage. You are all sincerely missed.

Last but certainly not least, to every woman who helped me reach my level, every muse, without whom I'd be hard-pressed to manufacture so many moments in time, adequately poeticized. You've contributed more than aware; this masterpiece is as much yours as mine!

About the Author

Corey Leigh is an emerging actor, author, and entrepreneur. He has long exhibited supreme talent and tremendous passion concerning creative arts. He attributes a love of literature to the means it provided him as a youth, a temporary figurative escape from the dangers of a troublesome urban environment.

A native son of Chicago, Corey is an esteemed alum of its prestigious Lane Tech High School. Additionally, he earned a bachelor's degree in Communications from Northern Illinois University. Successful in marketing and advertising, he has prioritized the pursuit of his vast creative ambitions above all.

As a writer, influenced mainly by Langston Hughes, James Baldwin, Ralph Ellison, Richard Wright, and August Wilson, he uses his creative skill to inspire and provoke thought, effecting positive change. Currently, he resides in Harlem, New York, drawing inspiration from spirits of its storied Renaissance.

www.ingramcontent.com/pod-product-compliance
Lightning Source LLC
Chambersburg PA
CBHW030554040726
47497CB00008B/2727